CROSSWIND

Land, Sea, Sky Book 1

Lynne Cantwell

Other books by Lynne Cantwell:

SwanSong
The Maidens' War

The Pipe Woman Chronicles:
Seized
Fissured
Tapped
Gravid
Annealed

Land, Sea, Sky:
Where Were You When: An Anthology
Crosswind

Indies Unlimited 2012 Flash Fiction Anthology (contributor)
Indies Unlimited Tutorials and Tools for Prospering in a
Digital World (contributor)
Indies Unlimited Tutorials and Tools for Prospering in a
Digital World, Vol. II (contributor)
First Chapters (contributor)
13 Bites (contributor)

For my fellow broadcasting refugees

Table of Contents

Chapter 1 1

Chapter 2 12

Chapter 3 19

Chapter 4 29

Chapter 5 37

Chapter 6 45

Chapter 7 54

Chapter 8 63

Chapter 9 71

Chapter 10 80

Chapter 11 91

Chapter 12 100

Chapter 13 111

Chapter 14 121

Chapter 15 129

Chapter 16 137

Chapter 17 146

Chapter 18 155

Chapter 19 162

Author's Note...171

Glossary 172

About the Author..173

Chapter 1

Tess gazed around her glitzy surroundings, feeling insignificant. She had worked in the news department at WWAS-TV for two years, but this was her first time at the Congressional Correspondents' Dinner. Until a few months ago, she had been a production assistant on the eleven o'clock news show and couldn't get off work to go. But now she was a writer for the morning news show. It had meant an adjustment in lifestyle – her circadian rhythm was still getting used to the midnight-to-nine-a.m. work hours – but at least she could attend the big party.

This wasn't the fanciest event for journalists in D.C. – that would be the more exclusive White House Correspondents' Dinner, also known as the "nerd prom" – but it was still a big deal. The vast main floor of the National Building Museum had been transformed into a banquet hall. Hundreds of round tables were covered in crisp white linen, and the chairs were beginning to fill with people Tess recognized: news anchors and reporters from the other local stations, network correspondents, members of Congress, and even some celebrities, all in evening dress. For a moment, Tess felt out of place, as if her Kansas farm roots were exposed along with her shoulders and slender neck. Sooner or later, she felt, someone would be along to kick her out on the street. She recognized the familiar anxiety and got a firm grip on herself. *Cut it out. You're a card-carrying member of this organization, complete with your very own congressional press pass. You have as much right to be here as anyone else. And speaking of....*

"Have you seen George Clooney?" she asked Tracie Kwan, the assistant producer for the noon news show, who sat next to her. She and Tracie had started at the station at about the same time, and the two of them had become good friends.

"No. Is he supposed to be here?" Tracie craned her neck.

"That's what I heard," Tess said. She admired Tracie's glossy, upswept hairdo, which had earned her some ribbing in the newsroom earlier in the day. Tess kind of wished she had Tracie's straight, black hair. Her own dark brown locks hadn't needed a hairdresser's care for tonight; Tess always wore her hair the same way – short and sculpted to her head.

"I don't see him. But this is such a big place, who knows? Hey, there's Antonia Greco!"

Tess turned in the direction Tracie was pointing. Sure enough, the host of "Talk About a New America" was threading her way through the tables, pausing to smile and shake hands with people along the way. Tess was surprised at how tiny she was; her natural charisma made her seem so much bigger. She was arm-in-arm with a Nordic god – blond and broad-shouldered, with chiseled features. "Ooh," she said, "she brought the senator with her."

"I'm not surprised," Tracie said dryly. "I heard she has to keep him on a short leash. Hey, are they sitting with us?"

Sure enough, the handsome couple had paused at their table and were consulting their tickets. "Table 67," the senator said. "That's us, honey." He glanced at the young women with a smile. "I guess we're table mates," he said, sticking out a hand. "Brock Holt from Colorado. You might recognize my wife."

"Of course we do," Tracie said smoothly, as Tess struggled to rise from her chair. "I'm Tracie Kwan, and this is Tess Showalter."

"Very nice to meet you," Antonia Greco said, shaking hands with them in her turn. "You both work for Channel 10?"

"Right," Tess said, finding her voice at last. "Tracie is assistant producer of the noon show, and I'm a writer for the morning show."

"It's a good show," Antonia said, turning to her with her hand outstretched. "We watch it every morning, don't we, dear?"

Tess took Antonia's hand to shake it, and felt her eyebrows rise. For a brief moment, the woman she saw before her was not Antonia Greco, but Diana, the goddess of the hunt. She blinked and the weird apparition was gone – but Antonia was looking at her a little oddly. Tess shrugged self-consciously and then averted her eyes, dropping the other woman's hand like a hot potato.

Senator Holt rescued the conversation. "I think I'll get a drink before they close the bar for dinner. Honey?"

"Oh, a glass of red wine would be lovely, dear." Antonia looked at Tracie and Tess. "Would either of you care for anything?"

Tracie raised her gin-and-tonic. "I'm set, but thank you."

"Tess?"

None for me, thanks, is what she meant to say. But what came out of her mouth was, "I'll have a glass of red wine, too." Antonia beamed at her as she reached down on the floor for her purse. "Let me get some cash for you."

But Senator Holt waved her off. "I've got it. My policy is to never let a pretty lady pay for her own drink." He actually winked at her as he turned away.

Tess felt her face grow warm. She couldn't bear to look at Antonia Greco – *the guy flirted with me, right in front of his wife!* – but Tracie gave her a raised eyebrow and changed the subject. "How do you like Washington, Ms. Greco?" she asked.

"Antonia, please," Antonia said. "Ms. Greco is my mother."

"Antonia," Tracie amended with a nod of thanks. "I thought you had a deal with the network to do your show from Denver."

"I did," Antonia confirmed. "And I loved it there. But once Brock won the Senate seat and we knew he'd be in Washington for at least six years, it just didn't make sense any more for me to stay there." She glanced in the direction her husband had gone. "I just felt like I needed to be here now." Her gaze drifted to Tess as she said, "For a number of reasons."

Tess got the distinct impression Antonia wasn't talking about her husband's roving eye. A crow croaked in her head; panicked, she dropped her eyes to her plate.

The first time she had heard a spectral crow, it had been chasing her away from the creek on her parents' property. It was right after she had refused an order from Morrigan, the Celtic goddess of war, to make an impossible choice: to hurt either her parents, or the multinational agriculture conglomerate that had taken their farm. It should have been an easy choice, but her father had just ordered her not to say anything against MegaAgriCorp and she was angry at him for silencing her. And too, she believed she was the sort of person who would never deliberately hurt anyone. Torn, she had fled, the crows mocking her indecision all the way home.

After that, the crow had sounded in her head a few times, always on the cusp of a big life change. And she always heeded the thing, even knowing she was playing right into Morrigan's hands. There didn't seem to be anything else she could do. Morrigan scared the hell out of her.

She chewed her lip nervously, wondering what the goddess had up her sleeve this time. As usual, she didn't have to wait long.

"So," Antonia said brightly, "do either of you have aspirations in front of the camera?"

"I don't," Tracie said. "I prefer being a producer."

Antonia laughed. "A control freak, huh? The best producers usually are."

"That's me," Tracie grinned. "Tess here, on the other hand...."

Tess knew a cue when she heard one. She swallowed her apprehension and said, "I'd love to be a reporter again. I was on the air in Pittsburgh."

Antonia looked impressed. "That's a good-sized market. A D.C. station wouldn't hire you?"

"It's just tough to break in," Tess said. "I could have taken an on-air job with the local cable news channel, but I wanted to work for a more stable operation."

"Good plan," Antonia said, eyeing her speculatively.

"Why do you ask?" That was Tracie.

"Oh. Well." Antonia leaned forward and spoke louder; the noise level was rising around them as people found their seats. "I'm thinking of adding a new feature to the show – an investigative unit, based here in D.C."

Tess sat up straighter. "I'd love to be involved with something like that. It would be great to have a job I could really sink my teeth into."

"Have you done investigative work before?" Antonia asked. Tess had, in fact, but she didn't have a chance to respond; the station brass joined them at that moment, accompanied by the eleven o'clock anchors, and another round of introductions ensued.

In the midst of the hubbub, Senator Holt returned with the drinks. His fingers lingered a split second too long against Tess's as he handed her the wine glass. This time, Tess risked a glance at Antonia; she was staring hard at her husband. Senator Holt finally noticed, cleared his throat, and sat down swiftly next to Tess.

Throughout the dinner and its accompanying polite chit-chat, the senator's knee kept brushing up against Tess's. At first, she thought it was accidental, and changed her position. She didn't realize he was doing it on purpose until the third time it happened; when she glanced up from her plate, she saw him looking right at her with an expression that bordered on a leer. She looked away immediately, half flattered and half astonished that he hadn't picked Tracie to flirt with instead.

As the dinner broke up, Tess excused herself in a hurry and practically ran for the ladies' room, mumbling something about beating the line. There, she hid in a stall for a few minutes to regain her composure. Tracie found her at the sink as she was washing her hands.

"What made you take off like that?" she asked.

"Senator Holt," she explained. "If my skirt had been shorter, I think his hand would have been up it."

Tracie's laugh was infectious. "I wondered why you were practically sitting in my lap," she said. "Come on, let's check out the after-parties."

Tess paused in the act of throwing away her paper towel. "What if we run into him?"

"We leave and go to another party. There are tons of them."

Tess was reluctant, but Tracie kept insisting. "Well, okay," Tess said finally. "But I have to leave by 11:30 so I'm not late for work." Together, they began making the rounds of the post-dinner receptions.

Every room was jammed; free booze was a great enticement. Tess kept checking the time on her phone. In one particularly crowded suite, she and Tracie immediately became separated, and as she was pulled farther into the room by the current of revelers, she wondered how long it would take her to get back out to the hallway. As she pulled her phone out again, someone jostled her and it slipped out of her grasp. She began to bend down to pick it up – but there was Senator Holt, scooping it up and handing it to her. "Oh," she said faintly. "Thank you, Senator."

"Call me Brock, please," he said, standing way too close. He had a beer bottle in one hand, and rested his other hand on her bare shoulder. "You're a lovely girl, Tess. I'd like to see more of you."

Tess was speechless – but only for a brief moment. The next thing she knew, Antonia Greco had come between them, breaking Senator Holt's grip on Tess's shoulder. "There you are," Antonia said, smiling grimly at her husband, who had the grace this time to look abashed. "I think it's time we headed home."

"I need to get to work myself," Tess told her, hoping Antonia could see the gratitude in her eyes. "It was very nice meeting you both."

Antonia slipped her a business card. "Nice to meet you, too. Send me your stuff," she said. "I mean it. Come on, Brock – let's go."

Tess watched them move away. But just as she was about to heave a sigh of relief, she had another weird vision. For just a moment, Senator Holt seemed to be bigger. The apparition surrounding him wore leather armor and a helmet with Viking-style horns on either side; it turned and winked at her just before the couple was engulfed by the crowd.

The crows started up in her head again. Tess resisted the urge to bat at the air around her ears and began to make her own way out.

Tess was utterly spent by the time she got home at ten a.m. Usually she ate a little something before she went to bed, but today she didn't think she even had the energy to pour herself some cereal and spoon it into her mouth. She parked in the back lot of the townhouse she rented with a college friend and, throwing the suit bag with her dress and heels over one shoulder, she dragged herself up the three steps to the kitchen.

The back door was unlocked, which surprised her. The coffeemaker was on and the carafe in it was half full, which didn't; Sue had a habit of forgetting to turn it off when she left for work. But what really surprised her was the presence of people in the living room at this hour of the morning.

She stopped dead, swaying a little, as Sue rose from the rocking chair by the front door. "Oh, good, you're home," she said cheerfully. "There's coffee ready, if you want some."

"All I want is to go to bed," Tess said bluntly. "What are you doing here?"

"I live here," Sue Killeen said, undaunted. "And Darrell here is thinking about joining us. Darrell Warren, this is Tess Showalter."

Tess groaned. She had forgotten all about the new-housemate interview Sue had scheduled for this morning. "Sorry, it's been a really long night. Nice to meet you, Darrell." She nodded to the man – trim, brown-skinned, dark-haired, serious military bearing – and resumed her journey to the stairs. "Just let me put this stuff away and I'll be right back down."

"Take your time," Darrell said.

The townhouse was an end unit with three bedrooms upstairs. Sue had the biggest bedroom, which overlooked the front courtyard. Tess's room was the middle-sized one – it was right next to the bathroom and had a view of the tiny backyard. The smallest room, in the front of the house next to Sue's, had belonged to Ginger, another college buddy. Ginger had been laid off from her retail job six months before. She had spent several months moping around the apartment, watching hour after hour of TV courtesy of Sue's

Hulu subscription, before announcing that she would move back to Texas. It had been a relief to Tess and Sue to have her gone – but without Ginger as a buffer, their relationship had begun to fray. Plus, Ginger's rent payment had gone with her. So Sue put up an ad on Craigslist, and Darrell had been the first to apply.

Tess hung the garment bag in the closet. Then she leaned against her desk chair and stared out the window for a minute, pulling herself together. It wasn't that Darrell was a guy – she and Sue had lived on a coed floor in their dorm at Georgetown – it was that she was exhausted. And she wondered whether he would be satisfied with Ginger's tiny room. She and Sue had almost ceased to think of it as a bedroom; they'd begun moving their extra stuff into the closet, and Sue had talked about converting it to a craft room if they didn't find a roommate. She wondered whether his shoulders would even fit through the doorway.

She shook her head. *What are you talking about? It's a standard-size doorway; of course his shoulders will fit. You need sleep, girlfriend.*

She gazed at her bleary-eyed reflection in the mirror above her dresser. She had put on makeup for the big dinner, and now her mascara was smudged under eyes, giving them a bruised look. *Or maybe I'm just that tired.* She sighed. *Well, suck it up, honey. The faster we get this guy out the door, the faster you can go to bed.* Sighing again, she took careful steps down the stairs.

"Coffee?" Sue invited again as she slumped into the swivel chair next to the stairs.

"How long have you been up?" Darrell asked.

Tess rubbed a hand across her eyes. "The dinner started at six, and I had to get ready, and then I had to get there.... What time is it?" She pulled her phone from her pocket. "Oh, God. Nineteen hours." She rested her head on the back of the chair and closed her eyes. "Go ahead, Sue. I'll stop you if I hear you say something wrong."

"And I'll lob a pillow at you if you start to snore," Sue said. Tess heard the snarky undertone and cracked an eyelid, but Sue had already moved on. "As I was saying, Darrell, we're used to shift work here, so your coming and going shouldn't be an issue. Tess works overnight at Channel 10 and sleeps during the day, and sometimes I work seven days a week, depending on the deadline for the project I'm working on."

"That's fine," Darrell said. "My hours vary depending on the project, too."

"Rent for this unit is twenty-nine hundred dollars a month, including utilities," Sue went on. "So that's a little less than a thousand a month for each of us."

Tess cracked both eyes open. That was more than Ginger had paid. If Darrell moved in, both Sue and Tess would save money.

"That's fine," he said. Tess was starting to like this guy a lot.

"Let me show you around," Sue said, getting up. "Tess, you don't need to come along."

Tess levered herself out of the chair. "No, I'd better. Otherwise I'll be asleep in a minute." She trailed them up the stairs.

Sue was motioning through the door of Ginger's room like the eye candy on a game show. "This would be your room," she said. "It's small, but it might suit you better than it would suit one of us – guys usually have less stuff, don't they?" She was smiling hopefully at Darrell as he ducked his head through the doorway. Tess, hanging back near the door to her own room, noticed that his shoulders did indeed fit through the door.

"Did you say you have a basement?" he asked as he stepped back out.

"I did," Sue said.

"I'd like to take a look at it."

They all trooped downstairs again, Sue pointing out the full bathroom and linen closet on the way. They wended their way through the living/dining room and the kitchen, past the half-bath, and down the basement stairs. Tess stopped about halfway down and sank to a seat, leaning against the cinder block wall, while Darrell prowled around the gloomy space, dodging boxes, castoff furniture, and their makeshift closet for winter clothing.

Finally, he said, "I can make this work."

Tess blinked and sat up straight. Sue said, "Wait a minute. You want to sleep down *here?*"

"Sure."

"But it's gross," she said. "It's damp, and there are spider crickets and Goddess knows what else. And the windows leak when we get a lot of rain."

Darrell had cracked a tiny smile – the first one Tess had seen on his face, she realized. "Goddess'?" he asked.

"Yes. I'm Wiccan. Is that a problem?" Sue said mildly, but Tess heard the edge.

"Not at all," Darrell responded. "Would it be okay if I moved all of your stuff to the bottom of the stairs? Then I could put up a partition with a regular door in it. I'd make sure to leave common access to the hot water heater and electrical box in the back."

"You'd have a huge space," Tess said, thinking aloud. "Like a studio apartment, except you wouldn't have a kitchen or a bathroom."

"Exactly," Darrell said. "I can shower at the gym at work, no problem. So all we would really be sharing is the kitchen and the half bath."

Sue and Tess looked at each other. "Sounds like a great deal for all of us," Sue said. "Welcome home, roomie." She and Darrell shook hands, and they trooped back up to the kitchen.

There, Tess held out her hand to Darrell. As he took it, she had another of those weird visions. This time, it was a giant rabbit's head superimposed over Darrell's. It grinned and winked at her, just as Senator Holt's apparition had. Tess blinked rapidly.

"Are you okay?" the rabbit asked.

"No," Tess said. "No, I am definitely not okay. It's been great to meet you and I'm glad this is going to work out for all of us. But I am so tired that I'm starting to hallucinate. If you'll both excuse me, I'm going to bed."

She could have sworn she heard the rabbit chuckling as she headed up the stairs. But what chilled her was the crow that cawed right along with him.

Milton Harkness awoke with a start. He checked the clock by his bedside: four-thirty a.m. He sighed, staring at the ceiling of his bedroom, tracing its irregularities in the near-darkness.

He had begun having trouble sleeping during his stint in prison. Even a minimum-security facility like the one he'd been in had its share of nocturnal interruptions. And too, he was never alone there; the bars may not have been as obvious as in a maximum-security facility, but the surveillance cameras were everywhere. Not once in the five years he was incarcerated did he feel able to fully relax.

Even now, five years after his release, he couldn't shake the feeling that he was being watched everywhere he went. He had a security company check over every inch of this condo for cameras and listening devices before he moved in; then he hired a second firm to do it again, just to be certain.

But he couldn't be certain. He could never be certain of anything anymore. Not since that ridiculous Second Coming.

He threw back the covers and went to the window. Pulling back the curtain slightly, he took in the view: the bridges over the Potomac, the Jefferson Memorial, the Washington Monument, and the U.S. Capitol beyond. Here he was, in the seat of power, and he had important work to do.

There was no one watching him, he told himself. Only God. The *real* God – not the impostor who those Indians had dredged up from somewhere to rescue that woman.

He had been right to kidnap her. He had been in the right to hold her until her demon child was delivered, and to silence it before it could fulfill its evil intent. That he had been judged by man's law had no bearing on the rightness of his actions. Oh, he had pretended contrition before the parole board; he had told them he recognized the error of his ways and that he would never trouble Naomi Curtis or her family again. He would have said anything to gain his freedom.

God – the *real* God – would forgive him the lie. He was sure of that.

But still, his life was in shambles when he left prison. His wife had already divorced him, saying she could never live with a man who could do what he had done to a pregnant woman. He tried to return to his old job, but the church elders, misled by the Indians' impostor, had seen fit to defrock him.

Night after dark night, he spent hours on his knees, sobbing. He had prayed to God – *his* God, the *real* God – to either give him a sign, or take him now.

Then one day, his phone rang. The caller offered him salvation: a job with a coalition of like-minded people in high places. He met with them, and found them to be kindred spirits. Not all of them believed in God – but to a man, they believed this new religious regime was taking America down the wrong path. Too much money was being spent on society's losers, too little was being allocated to keep America strong militarily, and too many restrictions were being enacted against the titans of industry who kept America running. It was becoming too hard to make money under this new regime. Why, there was even a movement to tax churches!

Harkness told them his belief: the Indians were at fault. They were the ones who stirred up all that trouble in Colorado in the first place. Somehow, they had escaped their proper place in God's Creation and were wreaking all this havoc.

The coalition heard him out, and then asked him to outline a plan of action. He spent several weeks crafting it. When he presented his plan to them, they accepted it.

He exulted. It was the sign he had prayed for.

The coalition had set him up in this apartment in Crystal City, overlooking the city Pierre L'Enfant had designed by divine inspiration. They were getting him an office on K Street, amid the high-powered lawyers and lobbyists.

And they gave him an assistant who was a True Believer, for all that she was a Catholic.

He turned back to the bed as she rolled over and peered at him, yawning. "Trouble sleeping again, Milton?"

"I'm afraid so, Heather," he said, sighing.

She raked back her abundant blond hair with one hand, pausing in a fetching posture. Then she patted the mattress. "Come back to bed," she purred. "I'm sure a little exercise will help."

Harkness thought of her creamy thighs parting for his steed, who was even now rearing in anticipation. Heather knew how to do things in bed no proper Christian woman should know, and she roused in him responses no Christian man should ever feel. But he was certain, as he crossed to the bed in two eager strides, that the *real* God – *his* God – would forgive him this, too.

Chapter 2

As Darrell filled boxes with his few worldly goods, he spoke to Someone who wasn't, technically, there.

"Explain to me why I'm moving into a place with two women and double the rent I'm paying now, and I can't even use the shower," he murmured. Neither of his roommates was home, nor did he expect them. But he wasn't inclined to risk someone overhearing him talking to himself – even if he wasn't.

For the fun of it? Nanabush responded.

Darrell's mouth turned up at one corner. "You do a lot of things for fun, but I'm pretty sure this isn't one of them."

Well, you've found me out. Nanabush was smirking. *I wanted to get closer to the redhead. If you know what I mean.*

"Sue?" Darrell said at full volume. "Oh, now, wait a minute. If You think You're going to set me up with *her*:..." He pictured Sue: tall and plump, with an earnest do-gooder air about her. She had said she worked for a nonprofit in Old Town Alexandria – getting farmers to put wind farms in amongst their crops, or something. Not like Ruthie at all.

Thinking of her *isn't going to do either of us any good,* came the mild rebuke.

"Stay out of my brain!" he said, not caring how loud he was.

I don't need to read your mind. All I need is to see the goofy look on your face when you think about her.

"Yeah, well," Darrell snarled, "if it hadn't been for You, I'd still be with her."

The Anishinaabe god sighed in his head. *It wasn't just Me. We've been over this, Darrell. I didn't make her take up gambling.*

Darrell shoved his books into a box, his mouth tight. Nanabush was right, as usual. When he had returned home to Dowagiac after Officer Candidate School, he'd found Ruthie at their tribe's casino, plunking coin after coin into the one-armed bandits. She quit – for him, she'd said – but when he came back from his last deployment, he discovered she was at it again. And this time, she refused to quit. Not even when he reminded her, as a medicine man, that a gambling addiction was not the route to the peaceful life all Potawatomi were supposed to be seeking.

Thoughts of his former life as a medicine man were another dangerous topic, though. Mentally, he shoved them into a box like the real one he was loading up with books, and sealed it with packing tape. Maybe someday he'd be ready to unpack that box.

Someday after all this was over.

He took a deep breath. "Let's try it again," he said aloud – but not too loud. "Why am I moving in with these women?"

Nanabush sighed in resignation. *Oh, all right. I forgot you can't take a joke.*

Darrell waited.

The god sighed again, and materialized in front of him. He looked human, mostly. He was dressed in deer hide, from His richly embroidered and beaded tunic, loincloth and leggings, to His moccasins. A few feathers stuck up from the roach clipped to His long, black braids. But the ears of a rabbit dangled from the sides of His head where human ears should have been, and His smile revealed rabbit-like buck teeth.

"Good," Darrell said. "Thank You."

Nanabush rolled His eyes. Then He got serious. "Things are coming to a head," He said. "These two women are on Our side, and you will need to work with them. We thought it would be easier if you all lived in the same house."

"'We'?" Darrell's eyes widened. "You mean they have gods running their lives, too?"

"I would have used a more flattering phrase," said Nanabush. "But yes, they do."

"And when Tess said she was hallucinating," Darrell said, remembering, "she wasn't, was she? She saw You, didn't she?"

The god only smiled, His buck teeth shining.

"Who *are* their gods, anyway?"

Nanabush's smile widened. "Goddesses. They're goddesses."

"So what did you see?" Sue asked as Tess stood at the stove, scrambling eggs for her meal-before-work. Tess had tried to figure out whether to call her first meal after a daytime sleep period breakfast or supper; eventually she'd decided that it didn't matter.

She scraped the eggs onto a plate and put the plate on the table on the other side of the pass-through. Then she walked around into the dining area with a cup of coffee and sat at the table beside Sue. "It was weird," she said, before digging into the eggs.

"How weird?" Sue was eating a tofu-and-veggie concoction that smelled better than it looked. Tess hoped there were leftovers she could bag up for her middle-of-the-night meal.

"Let me tell you about yesterday," Tess said between bites, "and then you tell me how weird *you* think it was." Sue nodded, and so Tess launched into the story about the correspondents' dinner — how Antonia Greco had looked like the goddess Diana for a split second; and how her husband, the senator, had come on to her, and then revealed himself to be allied with some Viking god. "So when I saw a guy with rabbit ears superimposed over our new roommate," she said, "I was pretty much done. What's the deal with him, anyway?"

Sue shrugged. "Officer in the Navy. That's all he said."

Tess sipped her coffee. "He looks exotic somehow."

"Cute, huh?" Sue said, smiling.

Tess shrugged. "He's okay, if you like a guy who looks like he's got a stick stuck up his ass."

Sue laughed. "Oh, come on! That's just the military thing."

"I've met plenty of military guys who look normal when they take off their uniforms. This one's got a stick up his ass." Tess began to giggle as she finished her comment; Sue's laugh was infectious.

"Well, I think he's cute," Sue said. "And yes, a little exotic. I'm dying to know what his story is."

"You'll have plenty of time to ask him after he moves in. Which is when, exactly?"

"He wants to remodel the basement before he moves any of his stuff here. He said he'd probably bring over the lumber this weekend."

"I hope he's not planning to bang around while I'm sleeping," Tess said. She stacked her dirty plate atop Sue's and carried them both into the kitchen.

"I told him early evening would be best," Sue said, following with the cups. "You want any more coffee? If not, I'll put your mug in the dishwasher."

"I got it, thanks," Tess said, rescuing the mug for a refill.

"So were you excited about meeting Antonia Greco?" Sue asked as she bent over the open dishwasher.

"Oh!" Tess's face lit up. She leaned against the counter. "Yeah, absolutely. And she wants me to send her some of my work. I'm so stoked. Working on an investigative unit for a network show would be, like, nirvana compared to what I'm doing now. I'm going to pull everything together before I go to work."

"Great." Sue grinned at her.

"But what do you make of all the weird stuff?" Tess asked her.

Sue straightened and shut the dishwasher. "I think something big is getting ready to happen."

"Duh," Tess said. "The question is what. Have you heard anything from Gaia recently?"

"No," said Sue. "Only the usual 'be prepared' stuff. You?"

"That's the other thing," Tess said slowly. "As I was going upstairs to bed, I heard a crow."

Sue frowned. "I didn't hear one."

"I'm not surprised," Tess said drily. "Gaia doesn't consort with crows."

"You think it was a message from the Morrigan?"

Tess shivered; she always did when she heard the goddess's name. "Possibly. Probably."

"But you didn't see Her. She didn't speak to you."

"Not yet, anyway." Tess shivered again, remembering the dry, harsh sound that accompanied the rabbit's laughter. That rabbit.... "So which deity is Darrell's, anyway? And who's the Viking? Any clues?"

Sue shrugged. "I'll have to do some checking. The Viking might be Loki."

Tess groaned, remembering the feel of Senator Holt's hand on her bare shoulder. "Great. That's just great."

It wasn't only the silent TV that had been a relief when Ginger moved out, Tess reflected as she powered up her laptop in her room that evening. The conversation she'd just had with Sue would have been a lot more difficult to pull off.

The three of them had lived on the same dorm floor at Georgetown. Sue was a year ahead of Ginger and Tess, and was eager to show the newbies the ropes. The three of them became best buddies, and when Sue's parents offered to buy her an apartment off-campus as an investment, she invited the two of them to move in with her.

It was certainly convenient, but Sue had hated it. The apartment was in what passed for a high-rise in D.C., and Sue complained constantly of the lack of daily contact with nature. "I want to see trees and grass when I look outside," she would say, "not just the sky. I want to be near running water."

"The Potomac's three blocks that way," Ginger had said.

"That's not what I mean," Sue had huffed. "Tess, you know what I mean, don't you?"

And Tess did, kind of. After all, she had had a creek of her own when she was a kid. So after Sue graduated and had been working for a while, she went looking for her own place. It had to be close to her job in Old Town Alexandria and not too far from the bustle of D.C., but with running water nearby. She'd found this rental townhouse complex in Alexandria's West End. It was close to I-395, but mature sycamores dotted the courtyards and Holmes Run was only a block away. She talked it up to Tess and Ginger, and they had both agreed to move in. Things had been great until Ginger lost her job.

Well, not entirely great. It was harder to talk about paranormal stuff when Ginger was around.

As a Jesuit institution, Georgetown had always required students to take religion classes. The Second Coming had obviously caused the school to overhaul the curriculum pretty rapidly, and some professors adapted more quickly than others. Sue still talked about what a pastiche her first-year theology class had been. The professor had thrown up his hands to some degree and brought in several guest speakers to talk about what they each thought it all meant. At least one of the guests had expressed disbelief that the Second Coming had happened at all.

Since then, opinions had solidified, with believers lined up on one side of the divide and deniers on the other. A lot of people straddled the line, though, even after the gods began interceding in daily affairs and making it plain that They meant what They said. Ginger wasn't to the point of being a full-blown denier, but she was certainly in the skeptical camp. "I imagine I'd find the whole story a lot easier to swallow if I actually knew someone who had been in contact with a god," she said airily one night when they all still lived in the dorm.

"You do," Sue said quietly.

Ginger laughed at her. "You? You mean that thing?" She pointed at a statue of Gaia that sat amidst candles and rocks on the top of Sue's dresser.

"Wait," Tess broke in. "I haven't heard this story."

"She had a *dream*," Ginger said in her Texas drawl, "full of *portent*." She waggled her eyebrows. Tess couldn't help but laugh.

Sue laughed, too, but she didn't say anything else. Tess changed the subject before Ginger had the chance to ask her whether she, too, had been approached by the gods.

But later, after Ginger had left for class, she said to Sue, "Tell me about Gaia."

Sue looked at her sharply. "Why?"

Tess sucked in a breath and said in a rush, before she could change her mind, "If you tell me your goddess story, I'll tell you mine."

A murder of crows cheered raucously in her head.

Sue stared at her. "Still waters run deep," she said. And then she told her how Gaia had come into her life via a Tarot reading on the day of the Second Coming. "Since then, I've visited with Her in meditation several times," she confided. "She wants me to be Her Right Hand when the time comes. Whatever that means."

"You deliberately seek Her out?" Tess asked, blinking.

"Well, not really, but.... Don't you talk to your goddess?"

"Not if I can help it," Tess said, and explained about the Morrigan. "So no," she said at last, "I don't seek Her out."

Sue tapped her chin with a forefinger. "Now I won't presume to tell you how to interact with your goddess," she began, "but it's my understanding that the Morrigan isn't always as bloodthirsty as is commonly believed."

Tess raised an eyebrow.

"Here," Sue said, turning to her laptop and pulling up a website.

Tess approached the computer. "That's Her, all right," she said of the image on Sue's screen.

"But see here?" Sue began paraphrasing from the site. "The Morrigan is also connected to sovereignty. In some legends, the king of Ireland had to mate with Her to ensure the fertility of the soil and, by extension, the success of the nation." Sue turned to her. "She's not just a goddess of war. She's an Earth goddess, too. Like Gaia."

Tess remained unconvinced. "So where does the war connection come from?"

"That's Badb," Sue said. "The Morrigan is three goddesses in one: Badb, Macha, and Anann. Anyway, the point is that the Morrigan is an Earth goddess as well as a goddess of war. So maybe She picked you because your parents were farmers."

"Maybe," Tess said uncertainly. "But She seemed pretty bloodthirsty to me."

The crows in her head agreed with her.

And they were agreeing again, now, as she pulled up the "Talk About a New America" website and clicked on the "Careers" link. They kept cawing at her as she uploaded her resume and the .zip file containing her best on-air work.

And they cawed at her again the next day when Antonia Greco called her, waking her out of a sound sleep, to offer her a job.

Chapter 3

The "Talk About a New America" operation was part of the New World News Network, whose studios were located in Southeast Washington, on a hill with a spectacular view of the Capitol and the Washington Monument. The site had been built out in the late 2000s for the headquarters of the Department of Homeland Security; in the decade since the Second Coming, as the gods convinced radicals the world over to drop their weapons or else, paranoia about a U.S. attack from abroad had eased. Consequently, Homeland Security's size had been ratcheted back, and the government had begun leasing some of the buildings on the site to non-government groups.

Prior to the Homeland Security tenancy, the site had been the home of St. Elizabeths Hospital, an institution for the criminally insane. One of the inmates had been John Hinckley, who had shot President Reagan in order to impress an actress he'd never met. Tess remembered hearing jokes when she first arrived in Washington about how one group of crazy people after another had occupied the place. She supposed some people would make the same joke today, now that NWNN was there.

It struck her, as she drove to her new job, how appropriate it was that she was starting on the day after Independence Day. She had high hopes that this network-level job would give her the career independence she had always craved. Now that she was away from Channel 10, she could admit to herself that working for the morning show had not fulfilled her. Too much airtime was wasted on stupid stories that didn't do anybody's lives any good. She hadn't gotten into journalism to write about celebrity babies; what she had always wanted to do was to find out the Truth, and to share it with others. Working for this investigative unit, she hoped, would give her that chance.

And it turned out Tracie felt the same way. When Tess told her she was leaving, the first thing out of Tracie's mouth was, "You'll need a producer." Tess realized that not only would she miss her friend, but that Tracie's talents, too, were wasted in local TV. So she screwed up her courage to call Antonia and suggest that she take them as a package deal. Much to her surprise, Antonia had agreed.

Tracie had just grinned and said, "She must want you bad. We should have asked for an extra week of vacation, too."

Traffic was light – a lot of people had decided to take the whole holiday week off – so Tess arrived in plenty of time for her first day. Most of the morning was sucked up in the usual new-job minutiae: getting an ID, filling out tax forms, and the like. She didn't get to meet up with Tracie until just before lunch, when their H.R. escort took them on a tour of the NWNN building, ending at the cafeteria.

He glanced at the line, and then at his watch. "How about I give you forty-five minutes for lunch," he said, "and then I'll come back and show you to the TAaNA studio."

"Sounds good," Tracie said, and the women got in line.

"What do you think so far?" Tess asked quietly as they surveyed the lunch options – healthier by far, she noted, than the sandwich joints and fast-food places that surrounded the Channel 10 studios.

"I don't know what to think," Tracie said. "It's a huge operation, isn't it?"

Tess nodded. She was still a little stunned at their brief view of Master Control, where the engineering staff monitored the NWNN channels that aired around the world. "Do you think we're ready for this?" she asked as she grabbed a plate of salmon and greens.

Tracie took a deep breath and let it out. "We'll find out pretty soon, won't we?" The women traded apprehensive looks.

The H.R. guy was true to his word. Forty-five minutes after dropping them off, he found them in the cafeteria and escorted them to Antonia's office.

Antonia was on the phone when they arrived, but she ended the call with alacrity and stepped around her desk to meet them at the door. Tess was struck again by how petite Antonia was; she was about Tess's height in her three-inch heels. Masses of dark curls framed her face. She wore a midnight blue silk dress under a jacket that matched her bright red lipstick. Her only jewelry was her wedding ring and a necklace whose pendant was a stylized bow and arrow.

Tess felt unprepared to see her in person again; they hadn't met face-to-face since the Correspondents' Dinner, and that had ended somewhat awkwardly. But Antonia was all graciousness.

"Welcome!" she said, clasping hands with Tess and Tracie in turn. "I'm so glad you're both here, and I can't wait for you to get started. I think this segment of the show will become a huge hit." She beamed at them. Tess smiled back uncertainly, and hoped she could live up to Antonia's assessment of her.

"Come on," Antonia went on. "Let me introduce you around."

The names whiffed by Tess; she hoped Tracie was retaining them. All she got were impressions. The producer was a bear of a man, with a blond beard and meaty hands. The newsroom manager reminded her of a whippet – thin, lanky, and a little nervous. She smiled at the writers, who barely looked up to wave, on deadline as they were.

Next Antonia showed them their office. Two desks had been crammed into a space meant for one, but Tess was in heaven. She and Tracie exchanged delighted glances. "A big whiteboard! And an actual door we can shut," Tracie said with glee.

Antonia laughed. "I thought you might appreciate being out of the newsroom bullpen," she said. "But I hope you'll keep the door open most of the time."

"Oh, absolutely," Tess said. "But it will be great when we're working with confidential information."

"That's what I was thinking," Antonia said. "And you're right down the hall from Pre-Production. Come on, let me show you."

TAaNA had its own three edit suites, all situated along a narrow corridor. Two of the rooms were occupied with tape editors hunched over their control boards, putting together segments for the upcoming show. But in the third room, a man sat with his feet up on the console, watching a soccer match on the monitor. "Heads up, Schuyler," Antonia said from the door, fighting a grin. "Your new crew's here."

Schuyler snapped to attention. "Yes, ma'am, Ms. Greco, ma'am," he said, saluting. "D. Schuyler Albright III, reporting for duty, ma'am!" Then he stuck out his hand to first Tracie, then Tess.

"Schuyler's your videographer," Antonia said, glancing at the clock above the monitor. "I've got to get ready for the show, so I'll leave you to get acquainted. You can watch from the control room, if you like. And afterward, let's talk about where we're going with this." She took off at a sprint.

"So," Schuyler said, "know any cute guys?"

Tess laughed in surprise. "Why, are you looking?"

"I'm always looking," he replied with a big grin.

Tess looked him over. He had sandy blond hair, light blue eyes, an engaging grin, and absolutely no fashion sense. "Not off the top of my head," she said, "but if I think of someone who swings your way, I'll let you know."

He seemed to collapse in his chair. "Story of my life," he said. Then he perked up. "So! Tell me about yourselves."

They spent a few minutes going over their respective work histories. It turned out Schuyler was also a Channel 10 refugee, as he put it, although he had left the station some time before Tracie and Tess came on board. They swapped stories about their former co-workers. Then Tracie asked him for the lowdown on TAaNA.

"It's great," he said. "And I'm not just blowing smoke out my ass because you're new. I've been here two years now, and I still love it. Antonia treats her people really well."

"Do you think she'll micromanage us?" Tracie asked nervously. "Seeing as how we're working on a new segment, and all."

Schuyler sat back and scratched his nose. "Well," he said, "I can't say for sure. She obviously has a vision of what she wants us to do, and the kinds of stories she wants us to go after. That's kind of her job, since she's executive producer and all. But I haven't ever seen her act heavy-handed with anybody."

"Comforting," Tracie said, trading a look with Tess. "I guess we'll have to wait and see."

"I guess so," said Tess.

Schuyler looked at the clock. "It's a couple of minutes before airtime. Shall we?"

As they left the edit suite, Tess asked, "So what does the 'D' stand for?"

Schuyler rolled his eyes. "Dwight," he said. "I hate it. Stupid family names. What's Tess short for?"

"Nothing," she said. "It's just Tess."

He sighed. "So uncomplicated. I envy you."

She smiled to herself. *Oh, Schuyler. If only you knew.*

Tess only half-watched the show. She was too busy watching a rapt Tracie as she watched the producer, whose name, it turned out, was Gil. He kept one eye on the clock and the other on his script, speaking softly into his headset to the anchors when they needed to cut a story short. Tess knew Tracie wanted a job very much like Gil's someday, and she hoped her friend would get her wish – but not before their investigative unit proved itself.

Afterward, Schuyler showed them to Antonia's office. He was about to drop them off when Antonia came up behind them. "Schuyler, why don't you stick around for this?" she suggested.

"Sure, boss lady," he said, and dropped into a chair. Tess and Tracie followed suit while Antonia shut the door. Then she shrugged off her blazer and hung it on a wooden hanger on the back of the door.

"Whew," she said, fanning herself. "Feels good to get that thing off. I'm always surprised when my makeup doesn't melt under the lights." She perched on the edge of her desk and frowned; then she pulled a chair over from the small table next to the window and sat in that. "That's better," she said. "So. Here's your first assignment.

"Over the past several months, we've been hearing chatter from the deniers. They claim to have inside information on how the Second Coming was faked."

"That's not new," Schuyler said. "We had a segment on it a couple of weeks ago."

"Right," Antonia said, "but those guys were obviously kooks. The chatter I'm talking about is more substantial. And then there's this." She reached for some papers on her desk and passed them around. "I've sent the email to your inboxes, but I know the two of you aren't set up on the system yet. We'll get that done before you go home tonight."

Tess looked over the news release. It purported to be from a group calling itself the Believers in the One True God – a.k.a. the True Believers – and announced a massive rally on the National Mall on August twelfth.

"I'd like to know who's behind this group," Antonia said. "Who's funding it and who's pulling the strings behind the scenes. If the answers are what I think they are, then we've got a bigger problem on our hands than just a bunch of conspiracy theorists."

Tracie looked up. "Who do you think is behind it?"

Antonia shifted and glanced out the window toward the Capitol. "I'd rather not say, in case I'm wrong. Let's just see what you find out."

"We can start on it now," Tess said.

Antonia shook her head. "Nah. It can wait 'til morning. Why don't you head over to your office now and start setting things up. I know you haven't had any time in there today, and I'm sorry about that."

"No problem," Tracie said. "It's only our first day."

"Uh, Antonia?" Tess asked, raising her copy of the news release. "What's our deadline?"

"No deadline," she said. "Just get the story. And keep me posted on what you find out."

"No deadline? Really?" Tracie asked, dubious.

"Well, I mean, before the rally, obviously. But I don't want us to report half the story, and then have another news outfit scoop us on the real deal. I want the whole enchilada." Antonia's words were light, but her tone was firm.

"Got it, boss lady," Schuyler said, getting to his feet. "One whole enchilada, coming up. With or without hot sauce?"

"With." Antonia grinned. "Definitely with. Now go on, get out of here. Go practice shutting your office door."

When the IT guy left, Tracie closed the door after him, grinning at Tess as the lock snicked shut. "Man, that feels good," she said, slouching into her seat. "Have we hit the jackpot, or what? A great boss, our own videographer, and an office with a door that shuts."

"And no deadlines," Tess said.

"It seems too good to be true."

"It does." Tess sighed and looked out the window. The view here wasn't quite as rarefied as Antonia's; their office was on the other side of the building from hers, and the foliage of a huge maple tree filled most of the window.

"So what do we know?" Tracie said, going to the whiteboard and writing *Believers in the One True God* across the top of the board in blue marker.

"Antonia said we didn't have to start 'til tomorrow," Tess reminded her.

"And?" She looked at Tess as if the answer were obvious. Then she picked up the news release, pressing the marker cap against her bottom lip.

Tess grinned at her and played along. "Their headquarters is on K Street," she offered.

"Not helpful. Three-quarters of the lobbyists in D.C. have offices on K Street."

"But it's a place to start."

"Yeah, okay," Tracie sighed and wrote the office address on the board. "I wonder what else is at that address."

Tess turned to her computer and started typing. After a moment, she sighed. "A dry cleaner, a sandwich shop, two fast-food places, and it looks like about a hundred lobbyists."

"Anybody else with that exact suite number?"

"No," Tess said. "Wait. Maybe. There's one suite number that's just one digit off." She looked up. "Don't building managers usually give each room in an office building a separate number?"

"I wonder if it's subleased?" Tracie said. "Hmm."

"We could go down there and check it out," Tess suggested.

"We could. We should call and try to set up an interview anyway. Whatever they tell us will give us more to go on." She went to her desk to reach for the phone, and then stopped. "Would you look at the time? This day has flown by."

"I guess we should go home," Tess said reluctantly. "It probably wouldn't do to put in for overtime on our first day."

The women looked at each other and exploded into laughter. "This is gonna be great!" Tracie cried. "I can't wait to come back tomorrow."

"Me neither," Tess said with a smile. "And I can't remember the last time I could say that about my job."

"Shut the door!" Sue yelled from the living room as soon as Tess opened it.

"What? Why?" she said, as two meowing kittens tumbled into view. "Hey, whose are those?"

Sue, wearing a delighted smile, followed them into the kitchen. "Mine. Aren't they adorable? The tuxedo cat is a boy – he's Puck – and the calico is Mrs. Norris."

"Uh-huh. Where did they come from?" Tess surveyed the critters as they batted at the tassels on her loafers. "Come on, guys, let me put my stuff down before you tear my shoes apart."

"You remember Pam, from work?"

"Um." Tess had a vague recollection of a middle-aged woman in a raincoat. They must have met at one of Sue's events.

"Her husband said the kittens had to go. So I said we'd take two."

"You're using the royal 'we' again, aren't you? Ow!" Tess reached down and plucked a kitten from her pants leg; it had dug its tiny claws through the fabric and into flesh in an attempt to climb her. "Look, you. No drawing blood. Here." She handed the black-and-white kitten to Sue.

"I thought you liked cats," Sue said, cuddling the little terror, who immediately swarmed up her blouse. "You said you always had them."

"Yes, but they stayed outside. I grew up on a farm, remember? My dad had a strict rule: if it had more than two legs, it didn't come in the house." She bent to pick up the calico, who was tumbling around her feet. The little thing snuggled down in her hand and began to purr. "How old are they? They look hardly old enough to be weaned yet."

"They're just weaned," Sue said. "Six weeks old."

"And how long have you known you were getting them?"

Sue smiled mysteriously and moved into the living room, the tiny cat over her shoulder. "They have a litter box set up in the bathroom down here, and one in my room upstairs."

"Uh-huh. And does Darrell know he's sharing his bathroom with them?"

"Not yet, of course," Sue said. "He's not home yet."

Darrell, it turned out, loved cats. Instead of making his dinner and heading downstairs with it as he usually did, he ate at the dinette table, then stayed in the living room all evening to play with the kittens. He even laughed several times, surprising Tess, who hardly ever got more than a slight smile of greeting out of him when their paths crossed in the kitchen.

"Did you have a cat, growing up?" Sue asked him as he dragged a string across the carpet for the kittens to chase.

"Always. And dogs. But as my parents got older, they stopped getting a new animal to replace the ones that passed on."

"It's tough to lose a pet," Sue said sympathetically.

Darrell nodded. "But when I was a kid, yeah, we had a series of dogs and cats." He looked up at her. "You?"

"Nope." Sue tilted her head toward Tess. "I was counting on Tess to tell me what to do, but she has no idea."

"That's not strictly true," Tess protested, expertly nabbing a furry body as it got near her. "I grew up on a farm," she told Darrell. "We had lots of animals. I know more than I want to know about taking care of them. But we never let the cats inside the house."

"Farm girl, huh? Whereabouts?" Darrell asked.

"Kansas. Near Wichita." She petted the calico kitten for a few moments, and then put it down. "Where are you from?"

"Southwestern Michigan," he replied. "A little town called Dowagiac."

"What's that near?" Sue asked frowning.

Darrell laughed. "Nothing. Well, South Bend, Indiana. We're pretty close to the state line."

"What did your parents do for a living?" she asked.

"Dad worked at an auto parts plant for a long time," he said. "He died a few years ago. Cancer."

"I'm sorry," the women murmured. Tess wondered whether it was grief that had made him so serious.

He shrugged. "He had a good life 'til he got sick. My mother is still there. She works for the...school system." Tess shot a look at Sue; she, too, had heard the pause.

"Sue's a local," Tess said.

"Nobody's a local in D.C.," Darrell said, one eyebrow raised.

"I am," Sue confirmed. "Born at Fairfax Hospital and grew up in Burke. Go, Lake Braddock Bruins!" She raised one fist and gave a self-conscious laugh.

"And your parents?" he asked, his attention on the kittens.

"Both lawyers."

"Ah," he said, and dropped the string. "Well. I should turn in. I need to be in early tomorrow." He levered himself up from the floor and bent to pet the cats in turn. Then he gave the women his usual smile and headed for the stairs.

"Darrell," Sue called after him. He turned, eyebrows raised in question. "I put a litter box in the half bath – is that okay with you? There's another one upstairs in my room."

He shrugged. "Sure. Goodnight." Tess heard him trot down the stairs and shut the door to his apartment.

She turned to Sue. "You should have gotten cats sooner. That's the longest conversation I've ever had with him."

Sue nodded, staring toward the doorway where he disappeared. "I wonder what kind of school his mother works for," she said.

"I'm guessing you'll have an opportunity to ask him soon enough," Tess said. "I have a feeling we'll be seeing a lot more of him."

"I have the same feeling." Sue focused on her. "Oh! I never thought to ask you how your first day went at the new job."

Tess felt her excitement return in a rush. "It was great. I think it's going to be everything I hoped it would be."

"Your big break," she said.

"More than that. I think we'll be able to make a difference."

"Good for you." Sue smiled politely.

"Antonia gave us a videographer," Tess went on. "She's terrific. Schuyler – he's our videographer – has been there for two years and he says he still loves working for her."

"Sounds great!"

"You have no idea what a videographer is, do you?"

Still smiling, Sue shook her head.

"Camera guy."

"Oh."

Tess rolled her eyes indulgently. "That's okay. I'll still be your friend. How was your day?"

Sue grinned. "I got kittens!"

Chapter 4

Two weeks after the kittens arrived, Sue knew no more about Darrell than she had learned the first day she'd brought them home. It was driving her crazy.

The more she saw of him, the more intrigued she was. He was handsome, she thought, with his brown skin and brown eyes. She knew he was an officer in the Navy – a lieutenant, according to the Wikipedia listing for the insignia on his uniform – and that he worked at the Pentagon. She knew he liked animals and that he was, apparently, an only child. And that was pretty much it.

He continued to spend some time with them every evening, giving the kittens a workout. He had found a seagull feather somewhere and brought it home for them to chase. Puck would make himself crazy trying to catch hold of it; Mrs. Norris was far more likely to sit and watch unless Darrell practically waved the feather in her face.

Which was why Sue was so surprised, early one Saturday morning, when Mrs. Norris paused at the top of the basement stairs, meowed once, dashed downstairs, and didn't come back up.

She considered going after the cat, but hesitated. Mrs. Norris would probably find a bug to play with, or something, and be back upstairs in a few minutes. So Sue finished making her breakfast.

No cat.

She sat down and ate it.

No cat.

She finished her coffee. Considered pouring a second cup. Went after the cat instead.

Darrell had pulled down the original partition that had divided the basement roughly in half crosswise, and had instead split the room lengthwise, with about two-thirds enclosed for his use. He had cleaned up the four half-height windows, two at each end, so that they actually let light in, and built his enclosure so that each part of the basement had two windows. There was a narrow passageway next to the stairs to allow maintenance access to the hot water heater in the back corner. Under the stairs, Darrell had built the women a closet with shelves, and he had also constructed a closet for off-season clothing storage in the front of the townhouse. Then he gave the whole basement a fresh coat of paint – even the floor, which was now dark green. Sue thought the new color was much more pleasant than the battleship gray they'd had when they moved in.

He had shown them all his improvements after he was finished. But he didn't show them his "apartment." And he made sure to move in his stuff when both Sue and Tess were at work.

Sue thought it all very odd.

So she descended the stairs with some trepidation, but also with a healthy dose of curiosity. Darrell, she knew, wasn't home; she had seen his car pulling out of the lot through the kitchen window as she'd entered that morning. And when she didn't see the cat after a cursory inspection of their part of the basement, and when she noticed that Darrell's apartment door was ajar, she only paused a moment before letting herself in.

"Mrs. Norris!" she called out, for form's sake. "Norrie! Where are you? You need to come out of here, Norrie. Come on upstairs with me." She looked over and under furniture – a sofa that had seen better days, a round table with a folding chair, several plastic crates' worth of books and movies – without success. Then she thought she heard a meow from beyond a curtained doorway to the rear of the apartment. "Norrie! Get out here!" she called again, and ducked through the curtain.

She stopped in surprise.

The room was chockablock with Native American motifs. An elaborate dreamcatcher hung from the rafters over the bed. A sort of shield hung on what appeared to be a closet door; a decorated drum held pride of place in front of a trunk that was draped with a tanned hide. Atop the trunk was a small charcoal brazier, an eagle feather, and several other items, all carefully arranged. A staff decorated with more feathers leaned against the wall next to the trunk. Hung over the altar – for she was certain that's what the display on the trunk was – she beheld an oil painting of a rabbit-eared man clad in richly-embroidered deer hide.

"What are you doing in here?"

Her stomach dropped. Trembling, she turned and faced Darrell, who looked murderous. "I was looking for the cat. For Mrs. Norris," she said apologetically, noticing, even in her embarrassment, how well he filled out the jacket and jeans he wore.

"So you broke in."

"No! The door was open! I would have never come in here if it hadn't been." It was clear he didn't believe her, so she kept babbling. "Norrie darted down the stairs all of a sudden. I waited a long time, but she didn't come back up. So I came down here to find her. And your door was open, and I didn't want to come in but I didn't see her anywhere on our side and I didn't want her disturbing your things...."

Darrell seemed to sag as her voice trailed off. "It's all right," he said, sounding defeated.

"So you're Indian," she said softly. At his nod, she said, "I thought all the Indians had to live on reservations out west. The Trail of Tears and all that."

"Not us," he said with a bitter smile. "The Potawatomi managed to convince the government that we were Catholic."

"Potawatomi? I've never heard of them. You." She risked a small smile.

"We're Anishinaabeg. So are the Chippewa – the Ojibwe."

"Oh! Louise Erdrich's tribe. I've read some of her novels. She's a great storyteller."

He nodded. "Our beliefs are pretty similar to the Ojibwe." He pointed his chin at the painting over the altar. "That guy, for instance. Nanabush. He's also known as Nanabozho, and a few other variations. The stories about Him vary, but He's always the same – kind of a doofus. And a Trickster." He said the last part ruefully. "I expect He's the reason my door was open."

Sue blinked. "I'm sorry?"

"He probably lured Mrs. Norris down here, too," he went on, as if talking to himself.

The kitten in question meowed inquiringly from behind Darrell. "There you are!" Sue said in relief, scooping up the cat. She turned back to him. "Well. I'd better go."

"Yeah." He didn't seem to know where to look.

She scooted past him. Then she paused at the curtain. "So your mom...."

"Works for the tribe," he said. "She administers some of the educational programming. Including the language school."

"Do you speak...Potawatomi?" she asked, hoping she'd said the name right.

"Yeah," he said. He gazed sadly at nothing, his thoughts obviously far away. Then he blinked and came back to himself. "Look, I'm sorry for all this," he said.

"For what?" Sue said. "You know I'm Wiccan, right? I have an altar of my own upstairs. I'd be happy to show you sometime." The invitation escaped before she could stop herself. She hoped he didn't think she was flirting – *come into my room and see my altar, heh heh heh* – but she admitted to herself that she wouldn't be upset if he did.

Darrell nodded. And then he said, "And Tess? What does she believe?"

Sue thought of the goddess who had chosen her friend – a goddess to whom, she was dead certain, Tess would never dedicate an altar or anything else – and said, "You'll have to ask her yourself." The words came out more harshly than she meant them to, so she followed them with a smile. Then she let herself out, closing the door firmly behind her.

"Thanks," Darrell said as he listened to Sue's footsteps crossing the kitchen above his head. "Thanks a hell of a lot."

"You were never going to say anything," Nanabush said from where He lounged on the bed. "I merely got the dialogue going." He leered at Darrell. "She's quite a dish, isn't she? And she likes you! 'Come up and see my altar sometime' – eh? Eh?" He studied Darrell's face for a moment. "Or is the short, skinny one more to your taste?"

"Shut up," Darrell said.

"I'm just trying to help," Nanabush said. "We need these women. And *you* need to forget about Ruthie."

"Shut up," Darrell said again, and walked out of the room.

"Tess! I figured out Darrell's story," Sue called excitedly from her room as soon as Tess opened her bedroom door.

"Wait...what?" Tess blinked. "Let me use the restroom first."

Sue waited somewhat impatiently. It had been a couple of hours already since her conversation with Darrell; she had spent the first hour or so searching the web for information on his tribe, and the rest of the time debating whether to drag Tess out of bed to tell her, or wait until she woke up on her own.

Within five minutes, a yawning Tess was standing in her doorway. "This had better be good," she said. "I need coffee."

"He's Indian," Sue said, grinning. "Isn't that cool?"

Tess squinted. "Native American, you mean?"

"Yes! Potawatomi. The Pokagon Band of Potawatomi Indians has its headquarters in that little town in Michigan where he's from. He told me his mother works for them."

"Cool," Tess said. "I'm going to get coffee, and then I'll come back up, and you can tell me how you found all this out." She disappeared down the stairs.

Sue turned back to the picture of Nanabush on her monitor. Then, smiling, she knelt next to the low table that served as her altar and lit a candle next to her statue of Gaia. She had a feeling things were beginning to come together, and that whatever Gaia's plan was, it would soon be revealed.

"So what's the plan?"

Morrigan regarded Nanabush with a supercilious stare.

"I mean," the rabbit-eared god said in the silence, "I've done My part. I've brought the three of them together. What happens now?"

Morrigan turned Her gaze to Gaia, whose expression was dreamy and unfocused. "Gaia!" She snapped.

"Hmm?"

"Our little friend here," She sneered, "asked You a question. And frankly, I would like to know the answer Myself."

"Oh. Well." Gaia focused Her sky-blue eyes on Her companions. "A convergence is coming."

"A convergence," Morrigan drawled. "What *sort* of convergence?"

"Earthpower," Gaia said, caressing Her belly.

Morrigan threw up Her hands. "Will You stop being cryptic and tell Us what We need to know?"

Gaia glared at Her sister goddess. "I don't know," she said. "If I knew exactly what was going to happen, I wouldn't need You two to help Me fix it, would I?" She glanced at Nanabush, who was staring at Her, mouth agape, and softened Her tone. "Oh, all right. Here is what I perceive: several Elemental events are coming together, starting in mid-August in Washington, the capital of the United States."

"Yes, I *know* Washington is the capital...." Morrigan began, rolling Her eyes.

Gaia held up a hand to stop Her. "These Elemental events," She went on, a trifle louder, "are likely to be the vanguard of a chain reaction. If left unchecked, I perceive – nay, I *fear* – that all Our hard work will be lost."

"That's a trifle dramatic, don't You think?" Morrigan said.

"Nevertheless," said Gaia, unperturbed.

Nanabush ignored the goddesses' bickering; He had grown so used to it that He was able to tune it out most of the time. "So this is it," He mused. "The attack We have feared, ever since Our hard-won peace agreement with Jehovah."

Gaia nodded. "And Our three human avatars, for lack of a better term, are in the best position to thwart it."

"But All signed onto the agreement," Morrigan said. "Even that troublemaker Loki."

"He's here, too," Gaia said.

"Whose side is He on this time?" Morrigan asked.

Gaia shrugged. "Who knows? His own, I suspect. As ever."

Nanabush nodded. "Nothing ever changes with that one. But if All signed – and that was My understanding, as well – then Who is stirring up the Elements?"

Gaia smiled at Him. "Think, Nanabush. Who was missing from the negotiation?"

Nanabush shrugged. "There were a lot of Us. I didn't count noses. Except for this one." He touched a finger to His own nose and grinned.

Morrigan, lost in thought, didn't appear to hear Him. She frowned at Gaia. "You don't mean Lucifer?" At Gaia's nod, Morrigan went off into peals of laughter. "But You can't be serious! He's not a god – he's some kind of...fallen angel, or something." Her hands fluttered for a moment before She crossed Her arms.

"Lesser beings have been promoted to godhood on the strength of a shorter resume than his," Gaia reminded Her. "All it takes is for enough humans to believe in him."

"Well..." Morrigan began, Her voice trailing off.

"But he's not a god," Nanabush insisted. "Or he wasn't, the last I knew. Hellfire and damnation have been falling out of favor with mainstream Christians for decades. All he's got are a few Satanists. And those snake-handlers."

"Alas," Gaia said, "he has picked up more since Jesus returned to Earth."

"The deniers," Morrigan muttered.

"Precisely. And the godless men of power. And all who seek to cause chaos for their own pleasure. Those who have lost the most since Our reign began."

"They are not actively worshipping him, though," Nanabush said. "The deniers, for one, believe they worship the true Jehovah."

"And who better to fulfill that role?" Gaia said. "The shift in power has given him an opportunity, and he is taking it. If We do not thwart him now, I fear We will be waiting longer than two millennia for another chance to restore balance." She stroked Her belly again. "And the Earth may not last that long."

"So it's war," Morrigan said, Her hand going to the sword haft at her side.

"Oh, well said! Well said!" A round of applause accompanied the sarcastic words. Loki, still clapping, emerged from behind Morrigan.

"What do *You* want?" She said, eyeing him.

"I want to help, of course." Loki spread his arms wide. "I stand before you a chastened Trickster. Finally, I have taken My rightful place alongside My brother gods and sister goddesses after My many thousands of years of exile. I knew when Odin pardoned Me that My reinstatement came with certain responsibilities – cooperation with My brothers and sisters being paramount amongst them.

"I couldn't help overhearing Your discussion just now, and as I happened to be in the neighborhood, and as I have a spot of unfinished business with some of the players in this Kabuki drama.... Ah, Nanabush," He said, grinning. "Good to see You, Sir! You are a rabbit after My own heart."

"Coyote said as much," Nanabush responded equably.

"You've spoken to Coyote? Then You've heard about Our clever victory over the Jaguar God." Loki smiled in satisfaction.

"He tells it a little differently," Nanabush said, stifling a grin. "I believe He said something about winning the battle, but nearly losing the war."

Loki waved one hand. "He has always been one to over-dramatize. So," He said, turning to the goddesses, "who's in charge?"

"Not. You." Morrigan glowered at him.

"Of course not! I am merely here to assist."

"Good." Morrigan's expression did not ease.

"Come and sit next to Me, Loki," said Gaia, patting the ground next to Her. When He had complied, She said, "No tricks, all right? None of Us will have time to do damage control."

"That's all in the past," He said, one hand raised as if swearing to it. "The only tricks I intend to play will be against Our adversary." Gaia stared into His eyes long enough that He threw up both hands. "Honest!"

Morrigan snorted. Loki glared at Her.

"And Diana?" Gaia asked. "Can We count on Her, too?"

"Of course," said the Huntress, joining Them. "And I promise that You need have no concern about Loki. Thor gave Me more than enough ammunition when He entrusted Him to Me."

Loki looked up at Diana, disgruntled. "Oh, that's perfect," he complained. "Rein in the old Trickster. Make sure He toes the line." He pointed at Nanabush. "What about Him, then? Who's keeping an eye on the Hare?"

Nanabush chortled. "Oh, please. I'm an amateur compared to You."

"The more important question," Morrigan said, "is who is keeping an eye on Our adversary."

Loki grinned. "Leave that to Me."

Chapter 5

Hart Senate Office Building, July 23rd

Brock sat up from the leather couch in his office and stretched. Then he shook his head to clear it. And here he had thought reading cases in law school was tedious; reading pending legislation, even when he was just skimming the executive summaries, was worse by several magnitudes. But coming in on a Sunday allowed him to get through it without phones or staffers interrupting him. He could show up in jeans, kick off his shoes, and get some work done. The only problem with the lack of distractions was that it was too easy to fall asleep.

He walked out to the office suite's pantry and started a pot of coffee. Then he slipped out of the suite and down the hall for a walk to clear his head.

The hallway was open on one side to the atrium. As Brock strode along, pumping his arms like a cross-country skier and noting his shifting perspectives of the Calder sculpture that rose from the atrium floor, he was surprised to hear voices floating up from a lower floor. Even more surprising was that the term, "damn Natives," came through loud and clear. He knew some of his Senate colleagues harbored a great deal of anger toward Native Americans; they were one of the minorities whose former treatment – or rather, mistreatment – was now getting what some Senators considered to be undue attention following the Second Coming. But the opponents didn't typically express their anger in a public place. Even on a Sunday afternoon, when the place was virtually deserted.

Let's get closer, Loki suggested in his ear. *See if we can figure out what they're talking about.*

Brock leaned against a pillar to rest, hoping he didn't look like he was eavesdropping.

"I understand." Brock recognized the voice as that of the Senate's president pro tem, Dick Gatlin from Tennessee. "But I can't sponsor that kind of bill. Not yet, anyway. It would be political suicide in the present climate."

"Well, just hold that thought, Dick," said the other man, whose Southern drawl Brock couldn't place. "Our group is working on changing the present climate. In fact, I wouldn't be surprised if the wind shifted within the next few weeks."

"What do you mean?" Gatlin asked.

"I mean that the coalition I represent is going to out those damn Natives, once and for all. All this namby-pamby stuff about loving your neighbor and living up to treaty obligations and not raping the land – that's all their double-talk, wrapped up in the message from that fake Christ who showed up in Denver a few years back."

He's a denier, whispered Loki unnecessarily; Brock had already figured that out.

"Why, I know for a fact that it was those damn Natives who found the guy to play Jesus for the cameras that day," the man went on.

"Who told you that?" Gatlin asked. Brock couldn't tell whether he was siding with the man or leading him on.

"Nobody told me. I was there! The whole thing was a setup! It was a con job set up by those filthy Natives and that woman lawyer."

Brock felt his anger rising. The "woman lawyer" had once been his fiancée. And while they were rarely in touch these days, he had developed a great deal of respect for Naomi Witherspoon Curtis and what she had been able to accomplish. Besides, he, too, had been in Denver when Jesus returned, and *he* knew for a fact that it had been the real deal. He considered finding the little toad and forcefully showing him the error of his ways.

Temper, Loki cautioned. *We don't know what they're planning yet.*

Brock nodded and swallowed his ire.

"Who's with you on this?" Gatlin asked.

"You'd be surprised," the other man said. His voice took on an oily sheen. "Two of your own colleagues and a Cabinet secretary, for starters. Bet you can't guess who."

"I've got an idea," Gatlin said.

So did Brock. If he'd been a betting man, his money would have been on Janet Karsten of Wisconsin and Rusty Dickens of Alabama. But the names he heard the unidentified man utter shocked him.

"Tyler, from Illinois," the man said gleefully. "Fred Preston from Montana. And your old pal Peter Magnon at the Department of Defense."

"I...." Gatlin was clearly speechless.

"Still waters run deep, don't they? We have a whole bunch of House members in our camp, too, from both sides of the aisle. So many see the danger. So many are concerned that those damn Natives and their bleeding-heart supporters will run this country right over a cliff!" The man paused, but Gatlin said nothing. "You just think about what I've said. In a little less than three weeks, all this is going to come to a head, and at that point, sir, the American people will need to know which side you're on: the right side, or the side of those damn Natives."

"Just a minute. What's happening in three weeks?"

"There's going to be a march on Washington, the likes of which this town has never seen," the man said. "We've reserved fleets of buses for church groups all across the nation to come here and march with us. We're going to fill the Mall for a rally with a record-setting crowd. And then we're going to...." The man paused. "Well, I can't tell you that. Not unless you're with us." Brock heard the man's voice fade slightly as he began to walk away. "I'll be in touch, Senator. In the meantime, you should be thinking about which side of history you want to be on."

Brock walked rapidly back to his office suite. There, he poured himself some coffee, went into his office, and shut the door. Then he called his wife.

Talk About a New America studios, July 24th

Tess's email beeped at the same time as Tracie's across the room. Tess saw the new message was from Antonia, and shared a worried glance with Tracie before reading it.

Come to my office, was all it said.

"Well, this is it," Tracie said mournfully. "It's been nice while it lasted. I wonder whether Channel 10 has hired anybody for my old job yet?"

"Please," said Tess. "They had somebody in your chair before the seat was cold." She stood. "Come on, we might as well get this over with. At least my resume won't be hard to update."

In the nearly three weeks since their investigative unit had been in operation, Tess and Tracie had broken a couple of stories. But they had made almost no progress on the story Antonia had assigned them on their first day.

It wasn't for lack of trying. Every day, they brainstormed another angle and ran it down; every day, it turned into either a dead-end or a brick wall. Even the phone number on the news release yielded them nothing; the pleasant receptionist who took their calls always promised to have someone call them back, but no one ever did.

The previous week, in a fit of frustration, Tess had dragged Schuyler on a wild goose chase to the company's office. The building existed, all right, but the room number belonged to a janitor's closet. And the building directory in the lobby had no listing for the Believers in the One True God – nor had they recently moved out, according to the security guard at the big desk in the lobby.

She and Tracie were well and truly stymied. And now the boss wanted to see them.

Antonia was at her desk, staring out the window, when they knocked. "Come on in and shut the door," she said. "Have a seat."

Tess blinked. Was that excitement in Antonia's voice?

"I think we may have a break in this thing," she said. "Senator Gatlin met over the weekend with a representative of an anti-Native-rights group. The representative was trying to talk Gatlin into sponsoring a piece of legislation favorable to the group's cause. He also said they're planning a big march on Washington in three weeks."

Tess consulted a mental calendar. "That's the same weekend as the deniers' group's rally. I bet it's the same event."

"I bet you're right," Antonia said. "My source unfortunately couldn't get a look at the man. But he did tell Gatlin the names of several senators and members of Congress who he claimed are supportive of his group's legislation. And he said the Defense secretary is backing them, too."

"Names?" Tracie said, and wrote them on her tablet. Then she sat back. "I have contacts on the Hill," she said. "I can probably get somebody to tell me whether any of these members have met with any deniers' groups recently."

"See if they have any meetings coming up, too," Tess said. "If this thing is going to be as big as this shadowy source claims, somebody's got to be managing the logistics. That means meetings."

"They'd need a Park Service permit, too," Tracie said. "That's public record. And the name of the organizer will be on the permit, complete with contact info." She exchanged a grin with Tess. "This could be our break!"

Tess's smile faded. "You know what? If these guys are not just deniers, but anti-Native-rights activists.... I wonder what's going on at the American Indian museum that weekend?"

Tracie tapped on her tablet for a few seconds. Then she sat back. "Their annual earth festival. They're going to have cooking and basket-weaving demonstrations, an art exhibit, and Native dance and music performances."

"The deniers wouldn't have the balls to try to disrupt the festival, would they?" Tess asked, turning to Antonia.

"They might," she said.

"Somebody needs to warn them," Tess said, thinking suddenly of Darrell.

"Well, we need to call them, that's for sure," Tracie said. "Somebody there may keep track of anti-Native-rights groups."

"The newsroom has some contacts," Antonia said. "Check with them."

Tess nodded and got up. "Will do. Thanks, Antonia. Come on, Tracie, let's get started."

Tracie flipped her tablet closed and slid it under one arm. "Hey, Antonia, you know what's funny? We thought you had called us in here to fire us."

"Oh, no!" She laughed. "But you've been doing a terrific job! The school funding exposé last week was brilliant. No, I knew this story would be hard to chase down when I gave you the assignment. I just hope this is enough to break it wide open."

"So do we. Thanks again." Tess grinned as she followed Tracie to the door.

Tracie turned the door handle and paused. "Hey, Antonia?" she said. "Tell your source we owe him dinner if this pans out."

Antonia blushed. "And here I thought I was pretty good at keeping a secret."

"Oh, you are," Tracie said loftily. "But we're crack investigative reporters."

Tess rolled her eyes at Antonia, who laughed softly as they let themselves out.

After dinner that night, Tess watched Sue play with the kittens and weighed whether to mention the Native American museum connection to the story she was chasing down. She and Tracie had made quite a bit of headway that afternoon: Tracie's friends on the Hill were combing members' calendars and lobbying contacts, and Tess had gotten the newsroom's anti-Native contacts and was slowly going through them for any sign they were connected to the march. Also, the Park Service had obligingly emailed them a copy of the permit for the march and rally. The name on the permit was the same as that of the contact on the original news release: Heather Willis. But the contact phone number on the permit was different. Alas, the same perky receptionist had answered the new number, and had assured Tess that Ms. Willis would call her right back. Tess immediately decided not to hold her breath.

Idly, she picked up a pamphlet from the coffee table and started flipping through it. "What's this?" she asked Sue.

Sue rolled her eyes. "It's contact info for everybody who graduated from high school with me. I don't know why they bothered to print out hard copies. They could have just emailed us all, or stuck it on a secure website."

Tess nearly put the booklet back down when a name caught her eye. "Heather Willis?"

Sue looked up. "What about her?"

"You know her?"

"I just said that we graduated from high school together. Weren't you listening?"

"No," Tess admitted. "I was thinking about how much trouble I've had getting hold of this woman."

Sue made a face. "Now why on Earth would you have any interest in talking to *her?*"

"Sounds like you don't like her much."

Sue went back to playing with the cats. "We had a falling out."

Tess's mouth quirked up at the corners. "High school drama, huh?"

Chin lowered, Sue looked up at her. "There was quite a bit more to it than that."

"Okay, okay. Jeez." Tess sighed. "It's too bad, though. I was hoping you'd call her for me."

"Oh, no. You can just get that thought right out of your head, missy. I have no interest in ever speaking to her again." She waved the seagull feather at Mrs. Norris, who yawned. "You little wretch," she said, with more vehemence than the cat's behavior called for. She dropped the feather and turned back to Tess. "What's this all about, anyway? Why are you so hot to talk to Heather?"

Tess told Sue as much as she could: about the information in the deniers' news release and the possible connection with an anti-Native-rights group. "This march or rally or whatever it's going to be is scheduled on the same weekend as the annual Earth festival at the National Museum of the American Indian," she said. "We're thinking they might try to disrupt the festival."

"Tell me the date again," Sue said, dismay dawning on her face.

"The march? It's August twelfth. The Earth festival runs from the eleventh through the thirteenth."

"And Earth Power Week is the seventh through the thirteenth," Sue said slowly.

"Oh, no."

"Oh, yes. And you're saying the Park Service issued them a permit for the Mall? They're crazy! We're going to have wind turbines and solar panels and experimental cars on display. We've even got a group coming in from Arizona to build a straw bale house. We can't have tons of people down there – they'll destroy all our exhibits! What the heck is the Park Service thinking?"

"Maybe their permit predates yours?"

"Not likely," Sue said with a short laugh. "We put in our reservation a year in advance. I'm going to have to call them tomorrow."

"While you're at it," Tess said with a sly grin, "how about if you call Heather and see if you can get her to talk to me? I can never get past her receptionist."

Sue glared at her for a minute. "Maybe it's a different Heather Willis. Did you ever think of that? What's the name of the group, again?"

"Believers in the One True God."

Sue shook her head. "No, that's her, all right." She sighed. "Hand me her number. I'll call her right now."

Tess waited expectantly as Sue pulled out her phone and punched in the number. "Hi, is Heather there?...Oh, hi, Heather. This is Sue Killeen. Bet you didn't think you'd ever hear from me again, did you?...Yeah, no kidding....Oh, you know, I saw your name in that booklet Francine felt the need to put together and...well, actually, now that you mention it, I do have an ulterior motive. Are you involved at all with a group called..." She looked to Tess for confirmation. "Believers in the One True God, I think it is....Uh-huh....No, no, I don't have any interest in joining." She laughed. "Yeah, I'm still doing that 'crazy goddess stuff.' Isn't that what you used to call it? But I have a friend who's been trying to get hold of you to ask you about this march or rally or whatever it is that you guys are planning next month....Uh-huh....Well, she's a journalist. Well, she works for Channel 10." Sue gave a thumbs-up to Tess's surprised expression. "Yeah, she'd like to come by and bring a camera guy, you know. Might be some good publicity for your march, right? Help the turnout?....Well, she's right here, if you'd like to talk to her now to set it up....I see. Okay, well, I'll see if that works for her, and if it doesn't, I'll call back and let you know. So where will you meet her? She said the suite number on the press release was a closet....Oh, sure, I know, typos happen....Okay, thanks, Heather, I'll tell her. Bye." She punched the button to end the call and said, "And she didn't even ask me what I was up to these days. Man, nothing ever changes with her."

"The appointment?" Tess prodded.

"Oh, right! Wednesday morning at ten at the Crystal Park Towers on Crystal Drive. They're moving offices, she said. That's why the press release had the wrong address. Plus her secretary typed the wrong suite number."

"Bullshit," Tess said. "They never had an office in that building. I asked the security guard when I was there." She shook her head slightly. "This whole thing just smells bad."

"What could happen at ten on a Wednesday morning?"

A number of dire possibilities crowded Tess's thoughts, but she refused to acknowledge any of them. Instead, she asked, "How come you told her I worked for Channel 10?"

"Stroke of genius, don't you think?" Sue said happily. "I figure she might be putting you off because you're from NWNN. 'Liberal media bias' and all that. But I know Heather – she's a local girl *and* an attention whore. She'd never turn down a chance to be on the local news."

"You may be right about that," Tess said. "I wonder if they'd loan us a camera."

Chapter 6

In the end, Schuyler sweet-talked the engineering staff out of a camera without the NWNN logo – a brand-new one that was meant to go to another show.

"It's adorable," Tess said, admiring the tiny thing. The omnidirectional microphone Schuyler was hooking to the top was almost bigger than the camera.

"It's several thousand dollars' worth of adorable," Schuyler said, sliding it into its case. "And I promised we'd get it back to them unscathed – or else 'True Tales of Milwaukee Wives' will take it out of either my paycheck or my ass, whichever they can get hold of first." He zipped the soft-sided bag shut with a little flourish. "Let's go, ladies."

"I'm staying here," Tracie said. "A local reporter wouldn't have a producer with her. And I've got some other stuff to do." She turned to Tess. "Do you still have your Channel 10 business cards?"

Tess held up a black plastic wallet. "And to think I almost pitched them the day I quit."

"Good thinking on your part. I did toss mine. Call me when you're done, okay? I'll be dying to know how it went."

The apartment building's foyer looked like the reception area of a high-end hotel. Tess suddenly felt out of place – dowdy, even, in her dark blue top, tan slacks, and cheap flats. It took all she had not to turn around and hightail it back to Kansas.

These mini-panic attacks happened to her only occasionally now. Back in high school, right after her parents lost the family farm to MegaAgriCorp, she would get three or four of them a day. The anti-anxiety drugs the doctor gave her back then helped, and time had eased some of the symptoms, too. But she still felt like a fraud on a fairly regular basis.

"You okay, Tess?" asked Schuyler. He was a couple of steps ahead of her; she must have stopped dead when the attack hit her.

She nodded. Then she took a breath and did the only thing that seemed to work reliably these days: she gave herself a mental pep talk. *You belong here. In fact, you DESERVE to be here. You work for a freaking network news show, and you're here to do your JOB – a job you're GOOD at. So put on your mask if you have to, but let's get this done.*

She visualized pulling a latex mask from her pocket and easing it over her head. Inside the mask, she could be frightened to death. But on the outside? On the outside, she was Network Correspondent Woman, Seeker of Truth.

Wearing her most confident smile, she approached the power-suited woman at the concierge desk. "Hi. I'm looking for someone named Heather Willis."

"You've found her," said a sultry voice behind them. Tess turned away from the concierge and beheld the woman approaching, one slim hand held out in greeting. Heather was tall and thin, with the build of someone who spends endless hours in the gym. Her shoulder-length blond hair was perfectly coiffed, her makeup was skillfully applied, and she wore her sleeveless silk dress like a second skin.

Tess hated her on sight, although she couldn't say why. Maybe it was the curl of her lip when she smiled; it put Tess in mind of a shark grinning as it circled its prey. Tess smiled back and handed her one of old business cards. *Just wait, honey. We'll just see who has whom for lunch.*

"There's a quiet place over here where we can talk," Heather said, pointing to an alcove off the foyer, where two armchairs were already facing each other. "Tell me," she went on as they sat down and waited for Schuyler to get set up. "How is Sue? I haven't seen her since the summer before college."

"She's fine. Oh, did you know? She works for a nonprofit, too – Earth in Balance."

"I think I've heard of it," Heather said, the lip curl out in force. "Aren't they the ones pushing U.S. energy independence by rejecting all of our most reliable energy sources? No oil, no coal, no natural gas?"

"I think Sue would describe it a little differently," Tess said smoothly. "And they're about much more than just energy independence, as I'm sure you're aware."

"Rawr," Schuyler said under his breath as he clipped the lavalier microphone to her shirt. Tess sighed inwardly and dialed back the cattiness.

"So tell me," Heather said, as Schuyler wired her for sound. "How did the two of you meet?"

"We were roommates at Georgetown."

"Ah." The lip curl became even more pronounced.

"Ready whenever you are, ladies," Schuyler chose that moment to say.

"I'm ready," Heather said, turning on a thousand-watt smile.

Willing herself not to squint, Tess tapped a couple of buttons on her tablet and nodded pleasantly. After another moment, Schuyler said, "And we're rolling."

"This is Tess Showalter, here today with Heather Willis, who is with the group Believers in the One True God. Ms. Willis, what is your title with that group?"

"I'm the executive vice president."

"And you're headquartered here in Crystal City, or...?"

"We're in the process of moving into the District."

"Ah." Tess looked at the notes on the tablet in her lap. "Can you tell me a little bit about your group? I had never heard of you before, to be honest. I guess you could say you're deniers?"

"We prefer the term 'True Believers,' but yes." Heather nodded. "We believe the Second Coming was faked, and that Jesus Christ has not yet returned. We believe the changes happening in our society due to that pseudo-event are against Scripture. We think America has gone soft as the result of this lie having been perpetrated on the American people, and we want to see our nation returned to greatness."

Tess glanced at her tablet again. "And this march you're planning – or is it a rally?"

"It's both."

"Ah. So the march *and* rally, then, will bring you closer to this goal? How?"

Heather was warming to her subject. "We anticipate tens of thousands of people will come to Washington on August twelfth. We will meet at the Washington Monument at nine a.m. and march down Independence Avenue to the Capitol, where we will hear from a number of speakers – including some members of Congress."

"Do you have a list of those speakers?" Tess asked.

"We're still pulling it together. I'll be sure to get it to you once it's finalized."

"Thank you. I'd appreciate it. So you say you have tens of thousands of people coming. Where are they coming from? I assume they're churchgoers, but are they from a particular denomination?"

"Oh, no," Heather said. "Our membership draws from many denominations – and many faiths. We even have some atheists."

Tess blinked. "Atheists who believe in the one true God? How does that work?"

Heather laughed. "They took one look at that fake Jesus and decided there's got to be a better way."

Tess laughed politely. "I see. So how big is your organization, in terms of membership numbers? A thousand? A few thousand?"

"Oh, no. We have over a million members." Heather nodded slightly, her eyes wide and her tone serious.

Lady, you are the worst liar on the planet. "And you're a 501(c)(3) corporation?"

"I'm not sure if that's the correct tax classification, but we're a nonprofit, yes. We're incorporated here in Virginia."

"Okay. So who's handling the logistics for the march and rally? Is that you?"

"Mostly, but I have a staff, too. And we have regional offices around the country. It's a lot like a political campaign, really." More earnest nodding.

"I see. So...." Tess looked down at her tablet again, although she knew exactly what she was going to say next. "Your group claims the Second Coming was faked, correct? I believe you said that earlier."

"Yes, that's correct."

"By whom?"

The tiniest of frowns appeared on Heather's forehead. "I'm sorry. I don't know what you mean."

"Who do you think is behind this big lie that's being perpetrated on the American people? What's the motive here? Who's behind it?"

On firmer ground again, Heather said, "We aren't sure exactly how the hoax was pulled off. But we suspect it was a coalition of liberal groups that enlisted Hollywood special effects experts to create the illusion that Jesus had returned."

"Like the moon landing?"

Heather laughed again. "Oh, now, don't try to lump us in with those crazies. Of *course* we landed on the moon. That was one of America's greatest achievements, and the kind of thing we'd like to see our nation achieve again."

I'll bet. And you'd cut NASA's funding in a heartbeat if its research doesn't turn up anything your backers can monetize. "So in your view, Native Americans didn't have anything to do with this fake Second Coming?"

The tiny frown was back. "I'm sorry?"

"Well," Tess said, "we've heard that another group – an anti-Native-rights group – is planning a big event on the Mall on August twelfth, too. And as I'm sure you know, it was supposedly a Native American goddess who convinced Naomi Curtis to mediate the agreement that preceded Jesus' return. Now, the Mall is a big place and it can hold a lot of people. But this just seemed to me like an interesting coincidence. I mean, here's this group, rallying against civil rights and fair treatment for the very people who precipitated the event that your group says didn't happen. And both of you are having big rallies on the Mall on the same day."

Heather's brows had knit together. "Where did you hear about this other rally?"

"Sorry," Tess said sweetly. "I can't tell you that."

Heather was silent.

"Any comment?" Tess asked.

"I didn't hear you ask a question," she said icily.

"Oh! You're right," Tess said. "I didn't. My apologies. Here's my question: Is your group, the Believers in the One True God, affiliated with this anti-Native-rights group, and are you working together on this rally?"

"We are the only group planning a march and rally in Washington on August twelfth," she said evenly.

"So your group is against Native rights?"

"I don't see how you could draw that conclusion."

"Well," Tess said reasonably, "if your march is the only one happening on the twelfth, as you say...."

"I just don't know where you're getting your information." Heather was visibly upset. She stood. "We're done here."

Tess glanced back at Schuyler, who was still rolling. "So you're not going to comment on whether your group is against Native rights?"

Heather unclipped the mic from her lapel, dropped it on her chair, and headed for the doorway.

"Oh, and Ms. Willis?" Tess called. "When you get that list of speakers firmed up, please send it to me here." And she held out her real business card.

Heather glanced at it. Then she looked at it again, harder, and shot Tess a murderous glare. "You lied to me!"

"Actually, it was Sue who lied to you," Tess said. "I just didn't correct her."

"I've been tricked into giving an interview under false pretenses!" Heather cried. "I refuse to allow you to use this material. Give me that camera!" She approached Schuyler, both hands extended, the fingers bent like claws. Tess tried to block her, but she shoved the shorter woman aside.

"Hey, you can't take that! It's NWNN property!" he yelled, hefting the camera high over his head. Heather was tall, but Schuyler had a longer reach. Heather stomped one elegantly-clad stiletto pump in frustration, and then body-slammed him. Schuyler lost his grip on the camera; it bounced against the wall behind him and landed on the floor.

"Oh, man," he breathed. "That's a brand-new camera. I hope you didn't break it."

"Give. Me. That. Video." She made to lunge past him, but Tess stuck out her foot and Heather went down, screaming and clutching her ankle.

The concierge appeared in the doorway, wringing her hands. "Is there something I can do to assist?"

"Call the police!" Heather screamed. "These people robbed me!"

The confused concierge looked at all three of them in turn. "But they're still here..."

"Just get some ice for her ankle," Tess said. Gratefully, the concierge departed.

Her perfect hair askew, Heather hoisted herself up into the chair Tess had been sitting in. "Give me that footage," she said again, "or I will call the police."

Schuyler was already picking up the camera. He looked through the viewfinder and sighed in relief. "It's still running. My ass is saved." He clicked it off and removed the memory card. "Okay, okay. Here you go," he said, dropping it into Heather's outstretched hand.

"What are you doing?" Tess cried. "You're giving her the interview?"

"It's okay, Tess, really," he said. "Grab the mics and let's get out of here."

Tess shot him a glare, but she picked up the mics and stuffed them into the camera bag. "Nice to meet you," she said to Heather, her voice dripping venom.

"Oh, it's been a pleasure," Heather said in the same tone of voice. "Tell Sue I owe her one."

Without another word, Tess picked up her tablet and shoved past Schuyler to the doorway.

He caught up with her as she exited the revolving entrance door. "I trust you recorded everything?" he asked quietly, tapping the tablet she carried under her arm.

"But of course," she said, with a sidelong grin.

Sue was having her own share of drama. She had spent a good chunk of the last two days on the phone with the Park Service, going several rounds over their permitting process. This time, she had managed to get through to the ranger in charge of the department. "Please explain to me," she said, "how you could have issued permits for two huge events on the Mall on the same day. Because I'm not sure I understand your rationale."

"Ms. Killeen," the ranger said, "I understand you're upset about this. But please believe me when I tell you that it's going to be fine. Your exhibit space starts across from the Washington Monument and stretches to Air and Space. The march will form up at the Washington Monument, and then move off Park Service property to march down Constitution to the Capitol. Your event will not be impacted by theirs."

"Until one of them gets a wild hair up their butt and decides solar panels are the devil's handiwork," Sue said. "You don't get what I'm saying here. These people are loony. They think the Second Coming was *faked*, for crying out loud."

"The First Amendment prohibits us from limiting the speech of any group," the ranger said stiffly. "We cannot deny a permit on those grounds."

"That's not what I'm saying," Sue said, smacking the edge of her desk for emphasis. "What if their crowd is bigger than they're projecting? What if the rally stretches back into our space?"

At that, the ranger laughed. "Ms. Killeen, if every denier in the *country* showed up to this thing, they wouldn't reach that far."

"Okay, but what about the other rally?"

The ranger paused. "What other rally?"

"Isn't there some kind of anti-Native-American rally planned that day, too?"

There was silence for a moment. Then Sue heard the rapid clicking of fingers on a computer keyboard. At last, the ranger said,

"There's a festival at NMAI that weekend. Is that what you're talking about? They're not going to be on the Mall — all of their events will be at the museum."

"No. I heard there was going to be a huge rally by an anti-Native-rights group on the twelfth."

She heard the ranger blow out a breath. "Well, if they plan to do it, they'd better get their application in soon. And if they plan to march to the Capitol, we're going to have to turn them down. That space is already reserved."

Sue sat back and rubbed her forehead with one hand. "Okay. See, that's what was worrying me — that we'd be talking hundreds of thousands of people down there, trampling our exhibits. If you say there's only the one group coming, then I guess we can work around them."

"Huh," the ranger said softly.

Sue froze, one hand still to her forehead. "What does 'huh' mean?"

"Well...it looks as if the permit application for the rally was amended and refiled sometime within the past week."

"Oh, really? What changed?"

"Well...they've upped the turnout estimate to a hundred thousand people. And they've added another sponsoring group."

"Who's the new sponsor?"

The ranger told her. Sue moved her hand from her forehead to her throat. She thanked the man and disconnected the call, and immediately called Tess.

"Dying to hear how the interview went?" Tess said archly. "I see why you stayed so close to your buddy Heather after high school. She's a real peach."

"Yeah," Sue said, not listening. "Look, you need to call the Park Service and get them to send you another copy of the rally permit. I was just told that they've added another sponsor."

"Oh, they did, did they? Who is it?"

Sue said miserably, "The European-American Rights Coalition. Only the biggest bunch of anti-Native nutjobs in the country."

"Shit," said Tess. "And the route of the march goes right past the American Indian museum. This is not going to end well."

Heather hobbled into the apartment and screamed, "Milton!"

Harkness turned away from his computer. "Oh, my dear," he said, hastening to her side. "What happened to you? Are you all right? Should we call a doctor?"

She waved off his concern. "Please tell me," she hissed, "if you can, how a reporter from NWNN heard about EAR-C?"

Milton reared back as if she'd struck him. "Not from *me*! I haven't told anyone except Senator Gatlin! And even then, I didn't name names."

"Well, they found out *some*how. Help me to a chair."

"Yes, of course, my pet," Harkness said, and put his arm around her waist. Once she was situated in the chair, he put some ice in a zipper bag and brought it to her, together with some painkillers. Only after she had taken the pills and iced her injury did he ask, "We're not going to have to cancel, are we?"

"Oh, no," Heather said, her lip curling in a smile. "Not at all. We're going to up the ante. They'll be expecting a big show now — and if that's what they expect, we'll be sure to give them one."

Chapter 7

Darrell's computer sounded a quiet bong. He looked around to make sure his commanding officer wasn't nearby. Confirming that the coast was clear, he clicked on the browser window.

Bozho, nitawes! Are you there?

Darrell smiled and typed back to his cousin. *Bozho, Mike! Ni je na?*

Can't complain, came the reply. *How's life in the big city?*

Darrell's expression softened. His relations had all been excited when he'd pulled this duty at the Pentagon. And it had been a relief to him, at first. He had needed the break away from the constant training-and-deployment schedule after the clusterfuck of his last mission. Besides that, he had tired very quickly of life aboard a naval vessel – everything was gray to him, even the food – and the long deployments had put additional stress on his marriage. But Washington....

Washington was where Ruthie had left him.

He sighed and replied with a lie. *Good. Working at the Pentagon is pretty cool. Can't really talk about it, though. How's everything at home?*

Good. Hey, we're going to be in your neck of the woods in a couple of weeks.

Darrell's eyebrows went up, and a smile dawned on his face. *Who's we?*

The dance troupe. We're going to be performing at a festival at the NMAI. Cool, huh?

Very cool! I can't wait to see you all. And he couldn't, he realized. He desperately needed a shot of his own culture.

Great! But there's a little more to it.

You don't need me to dance, do you? You know that would be a bad idea, cuz. Darrell chuckled to himself.

God, no! I know better than that! No, I was hoping I could talk you into doing a blessing ceremony for us the night before.

A lump formed in Darrell's throat. He typed, backspaced, thought, retyped, backspaced again. Finally, he typed: *Where's Gus gonna be?* Gus was a medicine man. He had been Darrell's mentor in another lifetime.

He's getting up in years, cuz. He doesn't want to travel anymore. He told me to ask you.

I left that life behind, Darrell replied. *He knows that.* And Gus knew why, too. Darrell felt his old, familiar anger rising, and tamped it down. It wasn't Mike's fault, or Gus's, that he was here in an office at the Pentagon instead of helping his people back home.

We all know it, Mike typed back. *But we can't go onstage without a blessing, and there's nobody else to do it.*

Darrell wrestled with himself. Part of him – the part he considered his true nature – sang joyously at this opportunity to be who he really was, if only for a few hours. Technically, he had never quit the Midewiwin; Gus had refused to let him. He had simply stepped away from the discipline.

Discipline. Medicine men were supposed to do a vision quest about once a year, and he hadn't been on one in ten. The last one had come to him unbidden, as he relaxed beside a creek at home, and had set him on his present path. He had been half-afraid to approach the spirits since.

Maybe it was time.

He glanced at the calendar, even though he knew it was Thursday. He had the weekend off, and he hadn't been camping in far too long.

Are you still there? Mike typed.

Darrell let his heart take over. *Yeah, I'll do it.*

That's great! I'll tell the troupe tonight. They will be so relieved. Iwgwien, midew.

Darrell flinched. He didn't deserve to be called a *midew* any longer. *Don't thank me until after the blessing,* he typed. *It's been a long time since I've done a ceremony. I might screw this one up.*

I have faith in you, came the reply. *I'll send you an email with our schedule. See you on the 18th, cuz.*

Bama mine, he typed in farewell, and shut down the browser. He went back to work, but his mind kept drifting to a tent in the woods, beside a rushing stream, with his cleaned catch sizzling on the fire.

"Going camping?" Tess asked him the next night, as Darrell plopped his loaded pack in front of the washer-dryer, next to the back door. She and Sue had finished their supper, he saw, and were cleaning up the kitchen. Tess was still in her work clothes – a short, fitted dress that accentuated her finer points – but Sue had changed into a tank top and baggy shorts, and had pulled her hair back into a sloppy bun at the nape of her neck. He couldn't help noticing, as he often did, the physical contrast between the two women, and wondered again how they had become friends. Sue was the Earth mother type, while Tess always made him think of a pixie.

"Yeah," he said, shooting them a brief smile. "It's been a long time. I hope I remember how."

"We used to camp a lot when I was a kid. I loved it." Tess smiled at the memory.

"You did not!" Sue said.

"Sure I did. Why is that so unbelievable?"

Sue plopped a freshly-rinsed dish in the dishwasher. "Because nobody really likes camping. Oh, people say they do. But if they really did, they'd be living off the grid, on some organic farmstead with the bugs and snakes." She shuddered, and Tess laughed at her.

"It's not for everybody," Darrell acknowledged. "But there are days when living off the grid sounds pretty good to me."

"It does have its appeal," Tess said softly. She glanced at him and looked away. He felt something turn over in his gut.

"Why don't you go with him, then, if you're so hot to go?" Sue said, one wet hand fisted on her hip.

"Maybe another time," Darrell said quickly.

Sue gave him an appraising look. "Ah. Secret Indian stuff, huh?"

"You could say that." He bent over his pack to adjust a strap that didn't need adjusting. When he looked up again, Sue had turned back to the sink.

"You know," she said over her shoulder, "we do outdoor rituals pretty often. Maybe you'd like to join us sometime. I think you'd be an interesting addition to the group."

He looked at Tess, who was staring at Sue. "You and Tess do rituals together?" he asked.

Tess snorted. "Oh, God, no. She's talking about her coven."

"It's not a coven," Sue protested. "Not really." She turned around and grabbed the dish towel. "It's just a group of like-minded people who get together and, y'know, celebrate the sabbats and esbats together."

"And do magic," Tess said.

"Earth magic," Sue shot back. "Everything we do is in service to Mother Earth. We don't do love spells and stupid stuff like that." She focused on drying her hands. "That stuff never works, anyway."

"Thanks for the offer," Darrell said. "I'll keep it in mind." He went back downstairs for his fishing tackle.

As he was about to start back up, he heard Tess say, "Why are you throwing me at him when you're the one with a crush on him?" He froze. He was sure he didn't want to hear this. He knew he should go back into his apartment and shut the door, and maybe even turn on some music to drown them out. But he knew they would be able to hear his door open and shut, and then Sue would realize what he'd heard.

And besides, Nanabush was now behind him, grinning and blocking his escape route.

He sighed to himself and hunkered down until the scene played itself out.

"I don't...I didn't..." That was Sue.

"Oh, please," Tess said. "It's written all over your face every time you look at him. I'm surprised he hasn't figured it out yet."

"Yeah, well, I'm surprised you haven't noticed the way he looks at *you*," Sue shot back.

Darrell's eyebrows rose. Did he? He remembered his gut fluttering at Tess's remark a few short minutes ago. Sure, he was attracted to her; she was cute, and he was male. But he was still in love with Ruthie. Wasn't he?

"What do you mean?" Tess was saying.

"Just now," Sue said. "He got all melty-eyed when you said you wanted to live off the grid."

"I don't want to live off the grid! What are you talking about?"

"You said it had its appeal."

"The *idea* sounds good sometimes. Don't you ever wish you could just get away from everything? Just disappear for a while and drop the mask and be who you really are?"

Darrell closed his eyes. The ache in her voice went straight to his own secret place. He wanted to cure her. No, it was more than that; he wanted to take her in his arms and grant her the safety she craved.

"I *am* who I really am," Sue said. "I don't need to wear a mask. And *you* wouldn't need one, either, if you'd just accept the Morrigan and be who She wants you to be!"

Morrigan? Darrell's eyes widened. In all the time he had spent with Tess, he had never had an inkling. He looked back at Nanabush, who wore a guilty expression. "Why didn't You tell me?" he whispered in a hiss.

Nanabush giggled and shrugged.

Fuck this, Darrell thought fiercely, and took the stairs two at a time.

Both women were red-faced when he burst into the kitchen, but he ignored that. "Okay, ladies," he growled. "Let's put all the cards on the table, shall we? I'll start." He turned back to the stairs. "Nanabush, get Your ass up here."

The lop-eared god poked His head around the door frame and waved. "Hi."

He turned to Sue. "Yours is Mother Earth, I presume?"

"Gaia," she nodded.

"Call Her."

"What?"

Darrell raised his hands. "What do you mean, 'what'? You can't contact Her?"

"I...uh...not without casting a circle...."

"We haven't got time for all that ceremonial crap," he said. "Get Her here."

"No need to call," Gaia said, floating up from the floor. "I am here. Hello, Nanabozho."

"Hi, sweetie," Nanabush replied with a cockeyed grin as He strutted up to Her. She rolled Her eyes indulgently at Him.

Darrell rounded on Tess. "Your turn," he said, aware of the menace in his tone and not caring it was there.

"I can't," she squeaked.

"I told you, we haven't got time," he said. "Call Her. Call the Morrigan."

"I can't!" she cried. She backed away from him until she was up against the sink, overturning the kittens' kibble dish with one foot. Tears stood in her eyes.

"She is not lying," a new voice said. Darrell turned; there was the Morrigan, clothed in black leather like some kind of Goth queen. She sat on the cabinet next to the washer-dryer, Her legs crossed at the knee. One booted foot swung rhythmically, tapping the edge of his backpack. He glanced back at Tess, who was practically cringing.

Later, he would allow himself the luxury of wondering about the history between two of them. Later, he was sure, his desire to take care of Tess would return, and he would call himself seven kinds of an asshole for this. But not now. Now, he needed answers.

"Thank You all for joining us," he said, allowing a little sarcasm to creep into his voice. "Would one of You mind telling us what the fuck is going on?"

"Well," Nanabush said, "We're all standing in your kitchen, and you're trying to order Us around."

"What makes you think you're in charge, manling?" Morrigan said.

He focused on Her. "Clearly, I'm not," he said evenly. "Or I wouldn't be asking You what the fuck is going on. Now, I already don't like You much. You've scared the shit out of Tess, and as far as I can tell, she hasn't done anything to deserve it."

That sent Morrigan off in peals of laughter.

"Darrell, don't," Tess said. "You don't know."

"I don't need to know," he said, not taking his eyes off Morrigan. "Not right now. What I need to know right now is why the three of us are here with the three of Them."

Morrigan slid off the cabinet and towered over him. "Who are you to question the ways of the gods?" She thundered.

"Do you want me on Your team or not?" he thundered right back.

Morrigan smirked. "I like this one," She said to Gaia. "Can I trade with the Hare?"

"No," Gaia said, but Her eyes were full of mirth.

"Oh, very well," said Morrigan. "Let's all sit down, shall we? It's getting a bit crowded in here." She led the group through the doorway into the living room, hooking one of the ladder-back dinette chairs with a finger as She went. She put it down with its back to the sofa and straddled it as the others took their seats: Sue in the swivel rocker by the front door, Gaia on the footstool in front of the rocker, Darrell and Nanabush on the sofa, and Tess on the bottom stair with her back against the wall. Darrell motioned her to the seat next to him on the sofa, but she shook her head and stayed put. He got the impression that she wanted to stay as far away from Morrigan as she possibly could.

If that's the way you want it, Tess, okay. For now. He turned to Morrigan. "All right," he said. "Talk."

Gaia sighed. "There is not much to tell that you have not already figured out," She said. "Yes, We brought the three of you together for a reason. As you said, Darrell, you are Our team."

"Against what?" He had transferred his attention to the Earth goddess, but he was having trouble keeping his eyes on Her face. The gown She wore was of some translucent stuff; the Earth She carried in Her belly shone through it, lighting up parts of Her body that a mortal man probably shouldn't be seeing. He shifted on the sofa, hoping his new position would hide his arousal.

It didn't – or at least, not fast enough. Gaia noted his discomfort and turned Her gown opaque. He felt his face grow warm and forced his focus back to the mission. "Against what?" he repeated.

"A convergence is coming," Gaia said. "Ten years ago, when We took control, We deliberately did not seek to punish every human who acted against Us. We knew it would be more effective for men and women to wonder when the gods would strike. Not every infraction was serious enough to require a thunderbolt out of the blue. And too, there are only so many of Us." She smiled ruefully. "Despite what you may have heard, We cannot be everywhere, all the time.

"We knew there was a faction of humanity that opposed Us. Some refuse to believe in Our message, preferring instead the perverted and judgmental faith they were brought up to believe was the true Word of God."

"The deniers," Tess said. Darrell noticed she had scooted along the stair to the edge closest to the rest of the group.

Gaia nodded. "Others," She went on, "refuse to believe in the existence of *any* gods, despite what they have seen and heard. Many of them held positions of great power and wealth during the lawless age before the Great Mediation, or they aspired to those positions. They did not want to give up their power. We understood why. We, too, had once held great power. We gave up Ours to Jehovah – and look where that got the Earth." She shook Her head. "But I digress.

"We thought Our initial efforts at fostering peace and caring would be enough to control this rebellion. We were sure that once Our opponents saw the Earth We were creating, they would understand, and they would join Us. But We did not realize how pervasive and stubborn their opposition was. We did not understand how closed their minds are to the Truth.

"And now, another is trying to capitalize on Our misunderstanding." Gaia fell silent. Darrell couldn't tell whether She was exhausted or dismayed.

He turned to Nanabush, who said simply, "Lucifer."

"Lucifer?" Darrell hooted. "The devil? Oh, come on. I thought we'd moved past this Good-versus-Evil crap."

"You don't believe he exists, do you?" Morrigan purred.

"Of course not. The devil was a Christian construct. God Himself said there's no such place as Hell." He glanced around the room. "Good versus Evil is a false duality. Everybody knows that."

"Do you know how gods come into being, manling?" Morrigan snapped.

"*I* don't," Sue spoke up. "Tell me. How do They come into being?"

"People believe in them," Nanabush said. "That's all it takes."

The goddesses nodded in confirmation.

Darrell digested this. "So Lucifer is a god?"

"Not yet," Gaia said. "Even after two millennia, he's only been able to attract a few worshippers. Most humans who rejected Jehovah, or Yahweh or Allah, stopped believing in anything."

"So he's not a god," Darrell said, "but he wants to be. So he's recruiting?"

"Not exactly," Nanabush said. "It's more like he's insinuating himself into the space between the deniers and the powerful. He's using himself as the glue that holds their alliance together."

"And you want us to break the bond?" Darrell shook his head at the enormity of the task before them.

"It's not as impossible as it sounds," Morrigan said. "You three have already uncovered much of his plot, with very little intervention from any of Us."

"The convergence point is August twelfth," Gaia said.

"The march," Tess said, sitting up straight. "No wonder EAR-C is joining up with the True Believers."

"EAR-C?" Darrell said, staring at her. "When did they get involved?"

"Just this past week. They're co-sponsoring the True Believers' march. And the route goes right past the American Indian museum."

"Shit," he muttered. "There's a festival there that day." He thought about his relations who would be there, and his anger rose.

"I know," said Tess, locking her gaze with his.

"It's also the next-to-last day of Earth Power Week," Sue said. She dropped her face into her hands and moaned, "All my exhibits are gonna be toast."

"Maybe not," Darrell said. He felt his resolve hardening as he spoke. "We have a pretty good idea of what they're up to. We have two weeks to prepare." He gazed around the room. "And we have the gods on our side."

Chapter 8

Tess went to bed early that night. As the adrenaline rush from her fear of Morrigan – not to mention being in the same room as *actual gods* – dissipated, she felt utterly spent. She was almost too tired to drag herself up the stairs to her room, and was certainly too tired to reopen the argument with Sue that had started it all.

But once she got in bed, she couldn't sleep. Sue's words came back to her: "The way he looks at *you*...all melty-eyed...."

And then he stood up to Morrigan on her behalf. To Morrigan! She didn't think anybody would be brave enough, or foolhardy enough, to stand up to the Irish goddess of war – especially after what happened to Cuchulainn.

In the months after her first encounter with the goddess, Tess had read everything about Her that she could get her hands on. The very first thing she found was the Irish tale called "The Cattle Raid of Cooley." In it, the legendary Irish warrior denied Morrigan several times when She took other forms to trick him, including once when She'd turned herself into a beautiful maiden and wanted to have sex with him. His denials had eventually cost him his life.

And She didn't just pick on Cuchulainn. Every Irish warrior was worried about meeting Her. If one spotted Morrigan beside a river, washing his clothes, he was sure to die in battle that day.

Maybe Darrell didn't know the legend, and so maybe he didn't know how much danger he had been in. She wondered if she should tell him. She wondered if she wanted to.

Oh, she cared about him the way she cared about any of her friends. Although "friend" might be too strong a word for her relationship with Darrell. Acquaintances, then. Or co-workers.

She turned over. Maybe "co-worker" was the best term, given their present circumstances. And she had made it a personal policy never to date a co-worker.

Well, okay. She had made it a personal policy never to date, period. Her career was more important to her than any relationship. She had seen women hamstrung by love. They began caring more about the guy than they did about their career, right up until they found themselves on the mommy track – stuck in a job going nowhere, rushing from work to pick up the kids at daycare and make dinner for the hubby. She had zero interest in any of that. She had focused on getting a network job; now that she had one, she was going to stay focused on keeping it.

Sure, Antonia had both a husband and a career, but you didn't see her pushing a stroller, did you? And she obviously had made other sacrifices. Tess recalled the senator's hand on her bare shoulder, and the way Antonia had looked at him. That whole scenario was not for her. No, if she didn't date, she would never have to worry about a straying spouse.

On some level, she realized she was unusual. Even in school, she wasn't interested in men, other than to chime in when somebody else talked about how hot some guy was. She could see how attractive the man was – she just didn't feel it.

Sue had speculated more than once about whether Tess was a lesbian. Except that Tess wasn't attracted to women, either.

She turned over again and glowered as she thought about Sue. Tess knew she desperately wanted to have a family someday, but she kept going for guys she thought she could fix. Or she'd fall head-over-heels for some guy who didn't suit her at all. Like Darrell, for instance. He was fit and handsome, and Sue was soft in all the wrong places. And then Sue would get pissed when the guy showed an interest in Tess instead.

Well, he *was* fit and handsome. Even if he didn't do a thing for her. Did he?

If she warned him about Morrigan, would he think she was coming on to him?

She turned over again.

Sue couldn't sleep, either. After Darrell disappeared downstairs and Tess fled up to her room, she sat alone in the living room, chewing over everything that had happened that evening.

Both cats had made themselves scarce while the gods were visiting. Now that the coast was clear, they came out and made pests of themselves. Puck jumped into her lap, nuzzling her hand so insistently that she got annoyed and put him down. He then stalked Mrs. Norris, who growled at him and ran. They chased each other around the room several times.

"Would you both please stop?" Sue said, her voice raised. But of course, it did no good. They only stopped when they had exhausted themselves. And then Norrie stood in front of Sue and complained at the top of her voice that Sue was in her chair.

"Fine," said Sue, and let herself out the back door.

Most of the neighboring townhouses were dark. Sue checked her phone and realized the park had technically closed hours ago. Still, she crossed Holmes Run Parkway and walked the half-block on the grassy verge to the entrance. Down the sidewalk she walked to the creek.

The sidewalk became a causeway as it crossed the creek; on the far bank, it met a steep concrete staircase up to the Holmes Run Parkway on the south side of the creek. Street lights lined the parkway, but the nearly-full moon gave her a better view of her surroundings. She made her way to a makeshift seat atop a boulder near the bank. There, she rested one hand on the pebbly soil and sent her thoughts down through it, searching for a seed. When she found one, she coaxed it to life. A few moments later, a buttercup bloomed right next to her hand.

Yet its cheerful beauty gave her no peace. She kicked off her flip-flops and moved to a boulder closer to the causeway, where she listened to the water crash through the gap underneath, its fury an echo of her jumbled thoughts.

She'd been right about Darrell's attraction to Tess. She was sure of it; she had seen the symptoms too many times before. And Tess was always oblivious. Sue couldn't even hate her for taking all the guys she herself was interested in, because she never *took* them. They'd fall down at her feet, and she would simply give them one of her distracted smiles and step over them. Eventually they'd decide she was a frigid bitch and move on. Occasionally, one would pour out his sorrows to Sue, and then she would have to play the understanding friend. By that point in the proceedings, even if the guy turned to Sue for sex, she was no longer interested. She knew she was the consolation prize.

The whole thing was maddening.

She picked up a rock and tossed it downstream with everything she had, but she couldn't hear the *plop* over the torrent next to her.

Every now and then, she would ask herself why she was still friends with Tess. Their interests had long since diverged – they didn't work in the same field, they didn't share the same passions, and Tess's unconcern over her lack of a love life drove Sue crazy. Ginger had served as a buffer between them, but now Ginger was gone. And Darrell's presence was just making everything worse.

She didn't want to think about Darrell. His strong arms, his ballsy move in standing up to Morrigan, the hard-on he'd gotten from his view of Gaia's breasts.... She smirked, thinking about how she could have helped him take care of that little problem.

Tess probably hadn't even noticed his erection. How could she be so *clueless?*

Well, anyway. She finally had an answer for why she and Tess were still hanging out together – they were supposed to be teammates against Lucifer. With Darrell.

She made her way back to the bank, where she paused in dismay. Her buttercup had wilted, its wiry stem now limp and its leaves shriveled. She pulled the remains from the ground and hurled it into the creek.

She hoped she could get through the next few weeks without bringing anything else to ruin.

Darrell, by contrast, had no trouble at all falling asleep. Years at sea – with its middle-of-the-night watches and unpredictable shifts – had taught him how to will his body into unconsciousness whenever the opportunity presented itself.

After a few hours, however, he was awake. He checked the time: 3:15 a.m. If he left now, he could be at the Atlantic Ocean by sunrise. He hadn't originally planned to drive as far as the ocean – after his last deployment, he'd decided that he'd seen enough salt water for a lifetime – but he surprised himself with a yearning to watch the sun come up out of the ocean like a ball of flame. So he levered himself up and, after a quick wash and a prayer at his altar, he shooed the cats away from the back door, loaded up the car, and hit the road.

It wasn't until he had crossed the Bay Bridge that he began mulling over the events of the night before. He wasn't worried about the coming battle with Lucifer. Because of Nanabush's interference in his life, he was now a trained and seasoned warrior. Battle tactics were nearly second nature to him; in fact, he had been somewhat dismayed to discover how easily such planning came to him. He remembered thinking at the time that no medicine man should be as competent as he was at waging war.

In any case, he wasn't concerned about what would happen on the twelfth of August. He needed more information, but that would come to him in time. Once he had a better picture of the lay of the land, so to speak, he would know how to proceed.

What worried him was the platoon he'd been handed.

He had spent enough time around Sue and Tess by now to know that there was something in their relationship that was fundamentally.... *Unhealthy* was the wrong word. *Unsound,* maybe. They had been friends for a long time, and roommates for nearly as long, and he guessed they were growing apart. Sue would sometimes look at Tess as if she wanted to strangle her. Tess, for the most part, was oblivious – which is why, he suspected, they hadn't had it out by now. Tess didn't think deeply about the friendship, so it just kept chugging along.

Actually, he hadn't believed Tess capable of thinking deeply about anything. Not that she was an airhead – far from it. But it had seemed to him that she cared only about her career, and she only cared about *that* insofar as it kept her from having to go back to Kansas. The fact that she had attracted the interest of such a complicated deity as Morrigan made him reconsider.

And what the hell had he been thinking, shouting down Morrigan like that? Did he have a death wish, after all?

No, it wasn't a death wish. It was that She was apparently in the habit of beating up on Tess, and his knee-jerk male response was to try to protect her.

And maybe even *that* let him off the hook too easily. Because if he were being honest with himself, he would have to admit that he'd had a hard-on even before he got a good look at Gaia's boobs. He'd had one from the first moment he saw Tess in that clingy dress. And it had only gotten worse when she talked about dropping her mask. There had been real pain in her voice – pain he was intimately familiar with.

That was why she skated along on the surface of life. That was why she didn't look too deeply into anything or anyone around her. She was scared to death of being vulnerable. Scared to death of being hurt.

And that, he realized, was the very thing the Morrigan was trying to get her to face.

He could relate to that, too. He'd shut himself away ever since Ruthie left him.

"Ah, now we're finally getting somewhere," Nanabush said in satisfaction from the passenger's seat.

"Get lost," Darrell said. "Haven't You caused enough trouble for one weekend?"

The god laughed as if He hadn't heard anything as funny in weeks. "See you in the Otherworld," He said, and popped out.

Darrell rolled his eyes and turned his attention to the road.

He had his sunrise breakfast on the beach, but it wasn't exactly what he'd hoped for. Ocean City didn't allow open fires on the city beach. So instead of home-cooked bacon and eggs, he had to settle for a fast-food breakfast sandwich. He refused to dwell on the number of similar small compromises he'd had to make in his life; instead, he enjoyed nature's light show and the antics of the gulls, and reminded himself that he was staying the night, and the sun would rise again tomorrow.

He drove to the Assateague Island National Seashore visitor center, paid for a backcountry permit, coated himself with sunscreen and DEET, and struck out along the shoreline.

Toward dusk, he emerged from his tent clad only in swim trunks and t-shirt. He walked to the shore and said a prayer. Then he shucked off the shirt and dove into the pounding surf.

When he emerged a short time later, he sat on the sand and closed his eyes.

He walked along the shoreline that he had hiked earlier in the day. The ocean and its breakers were on his left, and a wall of pristine dunes was on his right. If not for the tang of salt in the air, he could have been making his way along the shoreline of Lake Michigan.

He was overcome by a longing to go home. The light was different there; the sand, a finer grain. He was seized by the conviction that if only he could get off this endless beach, he could find his way home.

Obligingly, a path through the dunes presented itself. He took it.

On the other side was chaos.

Missiles lit up the night sky, cratering the town when they struck. Panicked people ran in all directions, seeking escape. A missile landed forty feet away; he scrambled behind the remains of a brick wall and crouched there, helmet to his camouflage-clad knees, just before it detonated. Body parts landed around him — some recognizable, some not. The stench of chemical smoke and roasted flesh hung in the air.

He looked back the way he had come, intending to flee, but the wall of sand dunes was gone. Instead, he saw the riverfront where his men had landed – and their landing craft going up in a blaze of light.

This was no vision quest. This was his last Special Ops mission in Syria. This was Al-Laqbah.

He and his men had been sent in to take out the local warlord and secure the village – a clean, surgical operation. But some moron higher up had ordered a drone strike on the same night. Hundreds of people had died, including most of the men in the platoon he led; out of sixteen men, only he, his second-in-command Terry Neiman, and two others had survived.

His familiar anger rose, just as it had then – anger and frustration at his own impotence, his own inability to save them all.

He knew he was having a flashback, and began struggling to force himself out of the trance. But Nanabush was beside him, anchoring him in the dream state. "You have to save them!" He shouted above the din. "Lucifer is behind this, too! All humanity is at stake!"

He stared at the deerskin-clad god in disbelief.

"Do something!" the god urged. "Go! Go! Go!"

Shaking, Darrell got to his feet. He looked down; he was wearing his fatigues no longer. Instead, he wore the ceremonial robe and headdress of a midew – the medicine man he had once been.

He did the only thing he could think to do. He raised his arms and prayed in his native language, beseeching Gitchi Manitou – the Great Mystery – to send these people peace.

When he reached the end of the prayer, he repeated it. And again. And because four is a sacred number to his people, he said his prayer once more.

As he prayed, he felt a breeze kick up around him. With each repetition, the winds grew stronger. By the fourth time through, they howled around him as if he stood at the center of a maelstrom.

When he had said his prayer four times, he lowered his arms and looked around. The drones had been blown away; the debris of war was gone. The people of the village, alive and whole, stared at him in wonder. His men – all fifteen of them – gathered around him, wide-eyed. He had ended the battle by faith alone.

Nanabush came up beside him and clapped him on the shoulder. He laughed uproariously at the shock on Darrell's face.

"I told you!" He crowed. "I said I needed both a warrior and a medicine man, didn't I? And you were it! Didn't I say that?"

Dumbly, Darrell nodded.

The rabbit-eared god whacked him on the shoulder again and said, "Am I ever glad that's settled. Now let's go back and get the women so we can kick that devil's ass!"

The first thing Darrell saw when he opened his eyes was the sun rising from the ocean like a phoenix.

The first thing he thought, after he had made his sunrise breakfast at last, was whether he could use his medicine to help Tess.

Chapter 9

Tuesday, August 1st

Sue pulled up in front of Denise's house at eight o'clock with a loaf of trendy bakery bread and a writhing gut. She had been assigned to bring the bread for her Wiccan group's Lughnasadh ritual. The apprehension was optional.

The group wasn't a coven; she hadn't lied to Darrell about that. A coven usually had thirteen members, and her group had only six. A coven also typically had a high priestess who conducted all of the rituals, and her group took turns. And a coven was usually dedicated either to the Goddess, or to the Goddess and the Horned God, and her group had members on both sides of the theological divide. Not to mention that she herself was pledged to a specific goddess, and not the Wiccans' Goddess, who was conceived originally as the Divine Feminine aspect that the Christian God lacked. Or at least, Sue knew, many Wiccans came into the religion looking for the Divine Feminine and found the Goddess.

It was all kind of complicated – but then, she had grown up Catholic, which was even more complicated. The lack of theological (or thealogical, if you wanted to get feminist about it) cohesiveness was partly due to Wicca being a fairly new religion. Its adherents had taken some flak for that in the early days – but all that stopped after the Second Coming. She remembered how delighted she'd been when those who groused about how Wicca was a made-up religion that hadn't stood the test of time (as if Christianity had never been new!) were reduced to making harrumphing noises when the Goddess actually showed up.

Not that She showed up a lot. The Goddess was very much a live-and-let-live kind of deity, and so She didn't bonk heads too often. There was the occasional drama-queen Wiccan who needed a quiet talking-to, but by and large, Wiccan faults were of the minor, getting-along-with-other-humans variety, which people tended to be capable of working out for themselves. At least in theory.

Her group met between eighteen and twenty times a year: for esbats, or full moon rituals, and sabbats, or the eight major holidays – the solstices, equinoxes, and cross-quarter days. Last year, they had conducted a handfasting; later this year, if all went well, they would do a baby-naming ritual for the same couple. They usually met at Denise's because she had a big backyard with a privacy fence. Wicca was a nature religion, so they celebrated outside if the weather was cooperative. In the colder months, and in summer when D.C. was graced with its typical stifling humidity, they would meet indoors instead.

This summer had been unusually temperate, although a wild rainstorm had driven them inside at the summer solstice and the May esbat had been stinking hot. The gods had done nothing Themselves to mitigate the effects of climate change, leaving it instead to humanity to do the job. Progress was, predictably, slow.

Today's weather had been beautiful, however — uncharacteristically cool and dry for August. And they had a twofer to celebrate: not only was it Lughnasadh, but the moon was full. So the group had foregone their usual practice of observing the sabbat on the weekend in the daytime, and decided to hold a moonlit rite for both.

She breezed through the side gate into the backyard, where Denise and Sammy were setting up the altar on a folding table. "All right! The loaf is here!" Denise said, and took the bread from Sue's hands to place it on the altar, near where ears of corn lay amidst a scattering of peaches and ripe figs.

Denise worked for the federal government; she had started out at the GS-4 pay grade and was now a GS-9 — "not bad money for a kid from Ward Eight," she had once told Sue. She had risen out of D.C.'s ghetto and had attended Georgetown with Tess, Sue and Ginger. After college, she had declined Sue's offer to move in with them, preferring instead to buy her own single-family house in Prince George's County, Maryland. Tonight, she wore a bright African-style dress and turban. Her mahogany skin glowed.

Sammy was younger than either of them. He was tall and a little gangly, with unruly dark hair and glasses with round lenses. Sue always thought that all Sammy needed was a scar on his forehead and the resemblance to Harry Potter would be complete. He worked for a government subcontractor as an analyst.

Now Becca and Tim emerged from the house through the sliding glass patio doors. Becca carried candles and a stack of plastic wine glasses, and Tim had a bottle of wine and another of grape juice. Becca's long hair was down, and she wore a flowing gown from which her belly protruded. Tim was dressed in the government lawyer's summer uniform: a dress shirt and khaki slacks. "No time to change," he said, gesturing at his shirt with the wine bottle. "Metro was a nightmare. I didn't get home 'til five minutes before we were supposed to walk out the door."

"I heard there was some horrible tie-up on the Red Line," Denise said.

"There's always a horrible tie-up on the Red Line," said Sammy. "I keep telling you guys, you ought to move to Virginia."

"Joanie's coming, isn't she?" Becca asked, changing the subject.

"As far as I know," Denise said, as the side gate banged. "Ah. There she is."

"Here I am," Joanie sang out. Her hair was a mass of curls, pushed back today with an orange headband. "And I brought blackberry pie!"

That got a round of applause. In response, Joanie curtseyed, holding the pie aloft on the fingertips of one hand.

"Gods, Joanie, hand that over before you drop it," Tim said, rushing to rescue the pie.

"Everybody got their sheet for the order of the ritual? I have extra copies inside," Denise said. "And do we have any additions?"

"Well," Sue said, "yeah. We do."

She had been working with this group for the last three or four years, yet she had never shared with any of them her connection to Gaia. Denise knew that she followed Gaia as well as the Wiccan Goddess and God, but Sue had never told her the extent of her commitment. Now, she had to come clean, and she wasn't sure how they would react.

She also wasn't sure whether she could count on them to help. While she considered these people her friends, it wasn't like she went out of her way to get together with any of them outside of group activities – not even with Denise anymore. She wasn't even sure they'd show up if she asked them to a party, let alone help her fight a war.

In the end, the only thing she could do was ask. So she gathered her courage and put it out there, and trusted the gods would give her the best possible outcome.

"I probably should have shared this with all of you sooner," she began.

"You're Catholic," Sammy said with a lopsided grin.

"I used to be Catholic," she said. "But y'all knew that, and anyway, that's not what I was going to say." She took a deep breath. "Besides the Goddess and God, I follow Gaia. In fact, She's kind of appointed me one of her soldiers, in a way." She looked around the group and saw respectful expressions, so she sucked in a breath and continued. "Okay. I think I may have told y'all about the festival that Earth in Balance is putting on later this month on the Mall. I found out last week that some other events are going to be going on at the same time." And gave them a brief description of both the NMAI festival and the anti-Native rights march.

"That's a problem," Tim said.

"Yeah, no kidding," Sue said.

"What can we do?" Denise asked. "I mean, we can certainly ask the Goddess and God tonight for Their protection and support for your project. But it almost sounds like you're after something more."

"I am," Sue said. "I have a feeling we're going to need all the help we can get on the twelfth. I was hoping we could conduct a ritual on the Mall, to try to make it a safe place for our festival and for the Indians, too."

Joanie frowned. "Not that I'm opposed to helping out," she said, "but the Indians have their own shamans. Can't they protect themselves?"

"Of course," Sue said, "and I'm sure they will. But this thing is going to be big, and I think they could use all the help they can get."

Tim and Becca shared a look. "We're supposed to leave for the Outer Banks on vacation that day. It's our last chance to get away before the baby comes," Becca said. "But I think we can delay our departure for a day."

"I'm in," Denise said. "Just let me know where to show up and what to do."

"I'll be there," Sammy said.

After a second, Joanie said, with a big smile, "Okay, sure. I'll come, too."

"Great," Sue said in relief. "I really appreciate it. We'll have some other help besides Gaia. There's Nanabush – he's an Ojibwe god – and the Morrigan."

Surprise registered on every face around her. "The Morrigan!" Joanie said. "You won't need us if *She's* going to be there!"

"Just who are we up against, anyway?" Denise said. "Besides the human nutjobs, I mean."

"Well," Sue said, knowing it sounded a little silly, "we think it's Lucifer."

"Lucifer?" said Sammy. "You're joking."

"And who's 'we'?" asked Denise at the same time.

"Tess. And our other roommate, Darrell."

Denise took a big breath, dismay plain on her face. "I don't even know that guy. And Tess is involved, too?" She shook her head. "We need way more info on this before we commit to anything, girlfriend. You go ahead and ask the deities for Their blessing during the ritual, but let's save the full discussion for Cakes and Ale."

Neither the Goddess nor Her consort made an appearance during the ritual, which disappointed Sue. She wondered whether it was because They didn't want to spook the rest of the group, or whether They weren't onboard with Gaia's plans, or what.

In any case, as Joanie cut the pie and passed it around, Sue went ahead and told the group what she, Tess, and Darrell had learned from their gods so far. As she spoke, she searched the faces seated around Denise's fire pit. Only Tim and Denise looked determined to help; the others' expressions showed varying levels of dismay. Joanie had actually shrunk back in her chair and pulled her knees up to her chin, as if to distance herself from both the project and the coming storm.

As Sue was winding down, Denise broke in and said, "You know, this is bigger than just us."

Sue blinked. "Well, yeah. That's what I've been saying."

But Denise was shaking her head. "That's not what I meant. This is going to be a big crowd, and there's only six of us. We're going to need more help with casting the protective circle."

"Who did you have in mind?" Tim asked.

"We can contact the people who run Pagan Pride Day, for starters," she said. "They can help us get the word out to other groups in the community."

"I know one of the organizers," Sammy said. "I'll send her an e-mail tomorrow."

"I can make some calls," said Becca, "but I don't know how much good it will do. If there's not going to be free love and free booze, we may have trouble attracting a big crowd." Her mouth curved into a tiny smile as she said it, and the others chuckled.

Denise grinned and said, "We'll just have to do the best we can." Her smile faded. "As I see it, this is a serious threat – not only to the Native peoples, but to the Earth."

"And to everything the gods have accomplished in the past ten years," Sue said, nodding.

"So we need to do our part," Denise said. "We've got less than two weeks to get it done. Okay, everybody? Tim?"

"You bet."

"Becca already said she'd help. Sammy, so did you." Each gave an affirmative nod. "Joanie, are you in?"

Joanie was silent, struggling with her thoughts. Then she said, "Lucifer's real?"

"Apparently," said Sue.

"But God said there's no Hell."

Sue closed her eyes for a moment. She understood Joanie's question; she had been there herself, not long before. "The Bible called Lucifer a fallen angel," she said. "Right? It wasn't until the Middle Ages that he acquired the horns and tail. And as we all know, because we've talked about it here, that didn't have anything to do with the biblical Lucifer. It was the Church's attempt to demonize the pagan gods, just as sage women became green-skinned witches with warts and pointy hats."

Tim said, "I think the most accurate depiction of Lucifer is the one in the story of Job." Sue settled back; she had heard him talk about this before. "It starts out with God and Lucifer sitting around, talking about how loyal God's followers were. Lucifer convinces God to visit a bunch of troubles on Job to try to shake his faith. Now, the Bible concentrates on how steadfast Job's faith is, despite his suffering, and how God eventually rewards him for it. The moral of the story is supposed to be to hold fast to your faith, no matter what tribulations befall you, and eventually you will be rewarded. Right?

"But for me, the most interesting role is Lucifer's. He basically goads God into taking a bet. From that, we can see that not even Jehovah is perfect. But we can also see how manipulative Lucifer is. I mean, he hornswoggled God! I think that's pretty impressive." Tim leaned back and slipped an arm around Becca.

"So he's not the devil," Joanie said. She had dropped one knee as Tim spoke.

"Right," Tim said with a smile. "The devil doesn't exist."

"But Lucifer does."

Tim shrugged and looked at Sue. "I guess so."

"It was news to me, too," Sue admitted.

"Well," Joanie said with a sigh, "I'll be there to help. But the whole thing scares me."

"I'm not exactly ready to charge in, myself," Sammy admitted. "But Sue needs us."

Becca didn't say anything, but her hands strayed to her belly. Sue smiled, noting the similarity of her movement to Gaia's habitual gesture.

"Thanks, everybody," Sue said. "I'm grateful that you'd even consider helping me. I admit that I thought twice about asking the group for support. My situation is different; I've more or less been drafted. Y'all are volunteers."

"But you need us," Sammy said again, as if that settled it.

"Okay, then," Denise said. "Today's Tuesday. Let's Skype Thursday night and see where we are."

Sue was buoyant when she got home. The ritual had gone well, despite the non-appearance of the Goddess and the God, and her group was mobilizing to help. She was whistling tunelessly as she let herself in the back door.

Tess sat in the living room, staring at some situation comedy on TV. She looked sideways at Sue, then sighed and hit the remote. The TV screen went dark. "Good meeting, I guess," Tess said heavily.

"Yeah, it was," Sue said, "and don't you dare try to bring me down. I guess your day wasn't exactly stellar?"

Tess tossed the remote onto the coffee table and sat back with a whump. "No," she said. "No, it wasn't."

Sue waited, somewhat impatiently, for the rest.

After a moment, Tess obliged. "We're just not getting anywhere with this story," she complained. "After Friday night, I thought it would be a piece of cake. I mean, we know who the players are now: Heather's group of deniers and EAR-C. Heather's not going to talk to us any more – I'm resigned to that. But we can't get hold of anyone at EAR-C, either. The one guy who returns our calls always promises to get somebody to call us back, but it never happens."

"You need a mole," Sue said, perching on the edge of the rocker. "An informant."

"Like Deep Throat?" Tess said, and gave a short, bitter laugh. "Here, let me just go out and recruit one."

"I know that's not how it works," Sue said. She felt her good mood slipping away by the second. "But you knew when you took this job that it wasn't going to be easy. Didn't you say that you were looking forward to doing real reporting? Working on stuff you could really sink your teeth into?"

"Yeah, I did," Tess admitted. "I just didn't know it would be this hard." She grabbed a throw pillow and hugged it to her chest.

"Well, I wish I could help you," Sue said, "but I don't know how I would."

"It's okay," Tess said with a sigh, setting the pillow aside. "I was just venting. See you tomorrow."

"Goodnight," Sue said, nearly tripping over a kamikaze cat. "Gods, Puck! Stop getting underfoot!"

Tess's giggle didn't improve Sue's mood. Puck led the way upstairs, nearly tripping her again. Partway up, she came level with a glowing pair of eyes on the other side of the iron railing. She reached through the bars and petted a purring Mrs. Norris. Then she trudged the rest of the way to her room.

Moonlight streamed in through the open blinds. As she undressed, she caught sight of her reflection, limned in silver, in the mirrored closet door – all belly and hefty thighs, or so it seemed to her. She frowned and swiftly donned her nightgown.

Sitting cross-legged before her altar, she lit a candle and sat back, trying to recapture the happiness she had felt earlier in the evening. The Goddess was unreachable, but perhaps Gaia would be there for her.

She found herself strolling along a woodland path. In another minute, she crossed a stone threshold and the woods disappeared. Now she was in a tunnel, winding down and down, into the bowels of the earth.

She arrived finally at a grotto. Stalactites grew from the ceiling, dripping water into the still, green pool below. Something in the pool's depths gave off a buttery rich luminescence that lit the whole cavern.

This was Sue's secret place – the place she retreated to when the world got to be too much for her. Sometimes she would meet Gaia here; this cavern was, after all, part of Her.

But today the goddess appeared to be elsewhere.

Sue sank down beside the pool and sought for her connection with the web of all life. She knew it was there; she had felt it many times before, the gossamer strand that tied her to every living thing, and every non-living thing, too. But tonight, the feeling would not come. Instead, she kept thinking of Sammy.

She knew he was in love with her. Once, during Cakes and Ale, he had imbibed a little too much wine and had walked her to her car, where he made a clumsy pass at her. But she just didn't feel that way about him.

No, when she imagined the perfect lover, it wasn't Sammy's image that presented itself to her. It was Darrell's – and he was looking at Tess.

Angrily, she tossed a rock into the pool, shattering the stillness and dimming the soft yellow glow. Then she sat, chin propped on one knee, watching the ripples slow and feeling very alone.

Chapter 10

The Pentagon, August 3rd

Darrell reviewed the meeting invitation from Commander Paulsen and frowned. The C.O. indicated he was forming up an ad hoc special-ops unit for a mission here in Washington. He scanned the list of recipients: sixteen men, all told, and every one of them had been trained as a SEAL. *What could you possibly need a platoon of SEALs for in D.C.?*

"Hey, Darrell," Terry Neiman said from the other side of his cubicle wall. Terry has been his number-two in Syria. "Did you get the e-mail from Paulsen?"

Darrell stood and looked over the top of the divider. "Yeah."

"Any idea what's going on?"

"No. And before you ask, it looks weird to me, too."

Terry shook his head. "I guess we'll all find out."

"I guess so." Darrell sat back down and accepted the invitation. When the time came, he and Terry strode to the conference room together and took seats at the front of the room.

Paulsen was already there. "Shut the door," he said, as the last man came into the room. "Men, we have a mission."

Darrell perked up. He'd been sitting on his ass in an office for far too many months now. His special-ops skills were getting a little rusty, and he was pretty fed up with doing paperwork. A practical drill was just what he needed.

But that's not what the C.O. had to offer them. "On the twelfth of this month," he said, "a large rally is planned for the National Mall. As you know, that area is under the joint jurisdiction of the Park Service, the Capitol Police, and D.C. Police. But we have been ordered to be on site and assist if needed."

Darrell glanced around at the slightly disinterested faces of his comrades. It was clear he was the only person in the room who knew which rally the C.O. was talking about. "Who issued the order, sir?" he asked.

"I understand the request" – the C.O. put a faint stress on the word *request* – "came through channels from a member of Congress."

Darrell just barely kept his mouth from dropping open. This was unprecedented, as far as he knew. Why would a congressman want a special-ops presence on the Mall? Were they expecting that much trouble? And who the hell was it who asked for the Pentagon's help?

"But that has no impact on our mission," the C.O. said. "Lieutenant Warren is in charge of the ground force, with Lieutenant j.g. Neiman as his second." Darrell heard several in the room suck in a breath; they all knew he and Terry had been at Al-Laqbah. Paulsen continued. "We will begin drills this weekend, so if you have plans, cancel 'em." He ignored the general groans and went on, "Muster is at oh-six-hundred hours Saturday. I'll have more information for all of you then."

"Uniform of the day, sir?" someone asked.

"No," the C.O. said. "Wear your civvies. We don't want to advertise our presence, or our plans. Dismissed." As the members of the unit saluted and filed out, the C.O. said, "Warren. Hold up a minute."

"Sir?" Darrell said. He exchanged a look with Terry.

"See you back at the ranch," Terry said, and filed out of the room with the rest of the men.

His boss waited until the last man was gone. Then he said quietly, "There's a logistical meeting for this thing tomorrow in Manassas."

"Sir?" Darrell frowned.

"It's at that megachurch out there off Prince William Parkway. Confidentially, I thought it was an odd location, too. Anyway, I need to go, and as you're the best tactician I've got, I want you to come with me."

"Aye, sir," Darrell said. "I'd like to find out what's going on myself."

"Good," the C.O. said. "The meeting is supposed to start at eighteen hundred hours. Damned inconvenient time, if you ask me, right in the middle of the dinner hour, and in kind of an inconvenient location, too. I plan to get an unmarked car from the motor pool and leave here at sixteen hundred. That gives us two hours to get out there."

"It's only a forty-five minute trip, sir."

"Not on a Friday afternoon." The C.O. shook his head again at the organizers' poor planning. "Anyway, be in my office tomorrow at sixteen hundred. Dismissed."

"Sir." Darrell saluted and headed back to his desk, his brain whirling. On one hand, he hoped the information about this planning meeting would help lift Tess out of her funk. She'd been moping ever since he got back from Assateague; Sue had told him it was because she was having trouble nailing down more information on the groups behind the rally. This might be the break she'd been waiting for.

On the other hand, he had a bad feeling about the whole thing. He wondered again who on Capitol Hill thought it would be prudent to call in the military on what ought to be a pretty routine civilian police matter.

He came upstairs as soon as he heard Tess come in the back door. "Hi," he said, poking his head out of the doorway and giving her a little wave.

"Oh, hey, Darrell," she said, glancing at him as she kept a weather eye trained on the cats. "No, Norrie, you can't go outside." She kicked half-heartedly at the calico, who yowled at her. "I'm not feeding you, either. Go talk to your mother."

"They've already been fed," Darrell said, scooping up Mrs. Norris and scratching her behind the ears. "Sue gave them dinner before she ran upstairs. Something about a status call."

"Really," Tess said. "Figures that they'd try to get a second dinner out of me." She sounded listless.

"Listen," he said, "I learned something today at work that might help you."

"Oh?" She opened the fridge and stared at the contents, sighed, and shut it again.

"Yeah. Um, do you need something?"

"Just dinner." She opened the freezer and pulled out an entrée, considered it briefly, and put it back.

"I brought home some leftover shrimp fried rice. It's yours if you want it," he offered.

"Thanks. I saw it." She shut the freezer door and turned to him. "What was the thing you heard at work?"

"Right. Well." He leaned against the washer-dryer and stuck his hands in the front pockets of his pants. "My unit has orders to help patrol the Mall during the rally on the twelfth."

"No kidding," she said, crossing her arms. "That's kind of unusual, isn't it? For the military to be called in?"

"It is," he confirmed, "and this is not a standard sort of order, either. Apparently a member of Congress put in the request."

"Who?"

"I don't know. But there's a planning meeting late tomorrow afternoon at a big church in Manassas. It stands to reason that some of the big players will be there."

She had perked up considerably, but her arms were still crossed. "Where did you find out about this meeting?"

"My C.O. has orders to be there, and he's taking me along," Darrell said.

She clapped her hands once, then squared her shoulders like a prizefighter. "Okay. I can work with this. Where and when?" She whipped out her phone and punched in the location and time. "I need to call Tracie," she said. "This can't wait 'til morning – she'll want to know now." Finally, a big grin overspread her face. It reminded him of the sun rising out of the ocean at dawn. "Thanks, Darrell. Thanks for this. You just made my week." Impulsively, she threw her arms around his waist and hugged him. By the time he could react, she was gone – reaching for her phone again and heading into the living room to make her call.

As quickly as she left, though, she was back. Hands on her hips, she asked, "Why is he taking *you* along to this thing?"

"Backup," he said instantly. "I'm supposed to take notes." Where that bit of subterfuge came from, he wasn't sure. Usually he didn't have a problem telling anyone how freakishly good he was at battle planning, but something made him hold back with Tess.

Her eyes narrowed. "And I suppose your notes will be classified."

He shrugged. "Nobody's told me that so far," he said. "Until they do, I'm an open book. Uh, that is..." he stammered, disarmed by the slow smile that spread across her face.

"You're cute when you're flustered," she said, and left again to make her call.

Tess's hands were trembling as she tried to find Tracie's number. *What the hell were you thinking? Hugging him?* Flirting *with him? "You're cute when you're flustered" – where the hell did that come from?*

Raucous cawing erupted in her mind, further unsettling her. But she managed to hit the correct button eventually, and began pacing the room, from the stairs to the front door and back, waiting for the call to go through.

"Hello?"

"Tracie! It's Tess. I've got good news," she sang. She glanced back to the kitchen; Darrell still stood near the back door, watching her, as if he'd turned to stone.

"This had better be really good," Tracie said. "I was just about to sit down to dinner."

"Six p.m. tomorrow at the Flame of God Megachurch in Manassas," Tess said.

"You're converting, and that's when you're being baptized," Tracie guessed.

"Of course not. That's the time and place for the next planning meeting for the August twelfth march," she said, suppressed triumph in her voice.

"Where did you hear that?"

"And that's not all," Tess went on. "Somebody in Congress has asked for the military to be on standby."

There was silence on the other end of the line for a moment. Then, "No kidding," Tracie said.

"No kidding."

"So...I think I know where you're getting your info now. Your source is reliable, right?"

Tess threw another smile Darrell's direction. "He hasn't failed me yet." She was rewarded with a slow grin in return.

"Okay." Tracie was all business, despite the fact that she kept pausing to chew. "We have no idea how late this meeting will go. ... So let's both get a good night's sleep and plan to be in at ten. ... I'll fill Schuyler in, and we can leave midafternoon."

"Why so early?" Tess asked. "Manassas isn't that far."

"I-66 on a Friday afternoon." Tess heard her swallow. "And also, I want to get the lay of the land before people start arriving for the meeting."

"Good idea."

"That's why I'm the producer," Tracie said brightly. "And now, I'm going to finish my dinner."

"Right. Enjoy. See you tomorrow." Tess ended the call and went back to the kitchen.

Darrell hadn't moved. Still kicking herself for her earlier effusiveness, she ducked her head. "Um. I did thank you for the tip, didn't I?"

"You did," he said, his voice a little unsteady. "But you could thank me again, if you want." Tentatively, he reached for her.

Surprising herself, she stepped into his arms.

They stood there together, her cheek upon his chest, until her stomach rumbled. Each chuckled self-consciously and they broke apart. "Sorry," she said.

"It's okay," he said. "I do still recommend the shrimp fried rice."

"I think I'll take you up on that."

Softly, with one hand, he stroked the side of her face. She wondered at his serious expression. Then he dropped his hand. "Well. Enjoy." And he disappeared down the stairs.

The croak of a single crow brought her back to reality. As she turned back toward the fridge, she stopped. Sue stood in the middle of the living room, anger and hurt etched around her eyes. Without a word, she wheeled and went back up the stairs.

Much later, Tess realized that she should have gone after Sue. And she would have, definitely, if her stomach hadn't chosen that moment to growl at her again. Instead, with a sigh, she began heating up Darrell's leftovers.

August 4th

Traffic was already beginning to back up on I-66 when Tracie, Tess and Schuyler got on from the Beltway. "I thought the Silver Line was supposed to make this better," Tess said, surveying the brake lights ahead of them.

Schuyler barked a laugh. "It did, for about fifteen minutes."

Grimly, Tess hunkered down and endured the stop-and-go ride. Eventually they reached their exit and headed south to the church.

The Flame of God Megachurch had been imposing when it was new; the building had stood apart, reaching for the heavens, back before all the land around it was developed into subdivisions and strip shopping centers. The front of the building remained grand, with its three-story windows of triple-paned glass and the stylized cross jutting up from the peak of the roof. A giant, spotlit American flag hung limp in the heavy afternoon air.

Typical August temperatures had moved into the area overnight, with humidity levels to match. Dark clouds massed to the west, but Tess almost hoped it wouldn't rain. She had lived in D.C. long enough to know that summer afternoon thundershowers usually made the humidity worse. "This stakeout is going to be miserable if we can't run the a/c," she said.

"It'll be fine," Schuyler said. "We'll keep the windows rolled down."

"You say that like it will help," Tess muttered.

"Come on," Tracie said. "Stop moaning. We haven't even started working yet. Let's go in and look around."

But they couldn't get in – all the doors were locked. They walked all the way around the building, trying every door, before giving up and retreating to the SUV.

"Just great," Tess said. "We don't even know which door they're going to go into, let alone where they're going when they get inside." She glanced at Schuyler, who was busily clicking away on his tablet. "What have you got there?"

He looked up, grinning. "The interior layout of the church," he said. "It's on their website." He pointed to the various doors. "The one on the far side of the building goes into the fellowship hall kitchens; I don't think we'll have to worry about anybody important going in that way. So that leaves the three sets of doors that we can see. The one on the left goes into the sanctuary, which they probably won't use; the one on the right is the back exit for the fellowship hall; and the middle one is for the church offices, meeting rooms and classrooms. If I had to bet money, I'd bet on them using that one."

Tracie nodded. "Makes sense." She looked up and pointed to a hedge planted along the building wall. "If worse comes to worst, we can hunker down behind those bushes."

"Yeah, well, let's head over there and get some food," Schuyler said, pointing to the shopping center next door. "It's already after five o'clock."

"Sounds good," Tess said. "And then we can park the truck near the dumpsters in the shopping center lot. We'll be hidden there, but we'll still have a good view of the door."

Less than half an hour later, Schuyler pulled the truck into the spot next to the dumpsters. "Now we wait," he said. The hand holding his burger stopped inches from his open mouth. "Well, lookee there. I believe we've got our first customer."

A dark blue government-issue sedan pulled into a spot in front of the middle door, and two men in camouflage fatigues got out. Tess scooted forward on the seat and leaned over the console between Tracie and Schuyler. "That's Darrell on the right," she said, pointing. "The other guy must be his commanding officer."

"He's your roommate?" Schuyler said. "He's a fine-looking hunk of manflesh."

"Pretty sure he doesn't swing your way," she said, giving him a sidelong look.

Schuyler shrugged. "A guy can dream. So who's this?" A red roadster had pulled in next to the Navy car; a moment later, three people got out. "Oh. Her," he muttered. One of the two was Heather Willis, the executive vice president of Believers in the One True God. Flanking her were two men in sober business suits.

"That's Jim Schulte on her left," Tracie said. "He took over as pastor here after they kicked out the crook – what was his name?"

"Dorfman or something," Tess said. The scandal was four or five years old now; Jesus Himself had shown up to throw the moneychanger out of the temple. "The other guy looks familiar to me, for some reason."

"Whoever he is, he's Heather's boy toy," Tracie said. And indeed, Heather was leaning into the man as his arm slid down from her waist to cup one trim buttock.

"Wait," Schuyler said, and began tapping on the tablet again. "I was right. It's the guy who kidnapped Naomi Curtis. Milton Harkness, formerly pastor of a church in Mississippi 'til he did time and they kicked him out of the ministry."

That one's clothes need washing, Morrigan hissed in Tess's ear. Startled, she looked around, but the goddess was nowhere to be seen. She was grateful to be sitting in the back seat; thankfully, neither Tracie nor Schuyler had noticed her jump. She reflected for a moment on how she would have explained it: *"Oh, well, see, the Irish goddess of war talks to me sometimes." Yeah they'd buy that, no problem.*

She refocused her gaze on the parking lot just as another car pulled in – a sleek, black sedan with government plates.

"Oho," Schuyler said, leaning forward. "And who have we here?"

"Holy shit," said Tess, both shocked and excited.

Three men emerged from the car, one after the other. The first was Senator Adam Tyler of Illinois. The second was Secretary of Defense Peter Magnon. And the third, who drew a hiss from Morrigan's disembodied voice, was Senator Russell Dickens of Alabama.

Tess watched them all shake hands as Rev. Schulte unlocked the doors. He let everyone in and pulled the door shut behind him. The black sedan circled the lot and left.

"Is that it?" Schuyler asked.

"Isn't that enough?" That was Tracie.

"Wait," Tess said, her eyes on the parking lot entrance as a nondescript sedan pulled in. "Looks like we've got one more."

This meeting attendee, too, had a driver. He was lean and fit in the same way Darrell and his boss had been, Tess thought, but the way he moved was harsher, more aggressive. He leaned against the driver's side door and spoke with the man behind the wheel. Then he entered the church while his driver, too, left.

"Another prime piece of manflesh?" Tracie asked Schuyler with a wicked grin.

He shivered. "No, thank you. That one looks like he'd castrate me."

"Anybody know who he is?" Tracie asked.

"No idea," Tess said, "but I've got the tag number. We can track it down tomorrow."

Tracie nodded and began eating her fries. Tess pulled out her sandwich, debated for a moment, and put it back in the bag. She was too keyed up to eat.

Rev. Schulte routed the attendees to a conference room in the megachurch's basement. A single long table, similar to the kind used in school cafeterias, dominated the middle of the room. Ten folding chairs surrounded it, four on each long side and one at either end. "Sorry about the lack of ambience," Schulte said with a smile, "but this is the most secure room in the building."

"It's perfect," Senator Dickens said. "Gentlemen and lady, if you please."

Darrell took an instant dislike to Dickens. The man projected plenty of charisma, but there was something off about him — something oily around the edges. Although, Darrell reflected, that might be true of every politician; he hadn't met enough of them to know for sure. Actually, Dickens and Tyler were the first.

Dickens took one of the head-of-the-table seats. Harkness sat to his right, with Heather Willis next to him. Darrell's C.O. sat down next to her, and Darrell took the last chair on that side of the table.

Tyler took the chair to Dickens' left; he struck Darrell as almost boyish, and perhaps an acolyte of Dickens'. Rev. Schulte sat next to Tyler, and they struck up some small talk; apparently their children had been on the same T-ball team. The SecDef sat next to Schulte. The late arrival, who Dickens had introduced as simply Quinn, slouched into the seat across from Darrell, propping an elbow on the table and fisting his hand over his mouth. At once, the SecDef leaned over and said something into the man's ear; Quinn's eyes danced.

"Let's get started," Dickens said. "First, thank you all for coming on somewhat short notice. I apologize for making y'all drive all the way out here on a Friday afternoon, but I felt strongly that we needed to meet away from the rarefied air of Capitol Hill and close to our base." He nodded in Schulte's direction. "Now, I've arranged for the commander of one of our military's elite special-ops forces to be here with us today, so let's go over our security plans, and then these boys can go home." He launched a grin toward Darrell's end of the table; Commander Paulsen gave a curt nod. "I suppose y'all are wondering," Dickens went on with a pronounced drawl, "why I asked for the Navy to send somebody over to help us out. Well, when you see this, I hope the reason will be clear. Milton." Dickens waved a hand at Harkness, who jumped, and then began handing around sheets of paper. "These are eyes-only, gentlemen and lady," Dickens said. "We'll be collecting them for the shredder at the end of the meeting."

Darrell saw Commander Paulsen frown, and glanced down at his own map. His eyes widened. *This is crazy!* The route of the march, from the Washington Monument to the Capitol via Independence Avenue, was marked in red. Black dots indicated where officers from the various police agencies would be located. And there was a blue line for his unit. It started at the bottom edge of the map and went up into the Tidal Basin, where it continued on land, heading east to the NMAI. There, it stopped.

"Senator," Commander Paulsen said, "what is this about?"

"Well, sir," Dickens said, "we're expecting a bit of a kerfuffle at the Indian museum when our people go by. There may be weapons fired and so on. So I asked the Secretary of Defense here for a unit that could handle itself in a war zone. He talked to the Secretary of the Navy, and that gentleman recommended your unit."

In other words, we drew the short straw. Darrell cut a glance at Magnon, who sat expressionless, staring at nothing.

"With all due respect, gentlemen," said Paulsen, nodding at Dickens and Magnon in turn, "this looks like nothing more than guard duty. My men are highly specialized warriors. To be frank, their training and talents will be wasted on this mission. Now, the District has a National Guard unit, and I believe they would be better suited for this."

"With all due respect, commander," Dickens sneered as he rose, "you have received a direct order, have you not?" He didn't give Paulsen time to respond. "I want your SEALS on the Mall because I want America to understand how big a threat these people are to our American way of life. And as the chairman of the Senate Armed Services Committee, I promise you that Navy special-ops funding will be in jeopardy if you disobey this order."

Paulsen's eyes had narrowed. "No one said anything about disobeying an order, senator."

"Good. I'm glad that's settled." Dickens resumed his seat. "Now, I want your men there to restore order and detain the troublemakers. We're after the element of surprise here. Nobody will expect a naval force to come sailing into the Tidal Basin. And Mr. Magnon tells me some of your boys were involved in that mission in that Syrian town. I read the report. Outstanding work against such long odds." He beamed.

For a moment, Darrell was back in Al-Laqbah, amidst the panicked civilians and death raining down from above. He shook his head slightly to dispel the memory. As he did so, he noticed the man named Quinn watching him with a measured look. Darrell held the man's gaze until Quinn's eyes flicked away. Then he tuned into the discussion again.

"Thank you, sir," Paulsen was saying. "But I still need some clarification on the mission you're proposing. I'm unclear why you believe you need 'the element of surprise' when you're dealing with your own protestors – who, as I understand it, will all be good, God-fearing Christians."

Dickens' next words chilled Darrell to the bone.

"You misunderstand," the senator drawled. "We don't want you to go after the marchers. The troublemakers we want you to deal with are the Indians."

Chapter 11

Tess hated stakeouts. Waiting around for something to happen was the most miserably boring exercise she could think of. The three of them had rapidly run through small talk about the weather (the consensus: hot), the summer movie season (lousy), and local music venues (Tess's vote for the Birchmere drew incredulous looks from Schuyler), and were casting around for something else to talk about when the church's door opened.

"Here they come," Tracie said, suppressed excitement in her voice.

Stomach fluttering, Tess hopped out of the truck and handed off the camera to Schuyler. Darrell and his boss, standing next to their car, looked up in surprise at Tess and Schuyler as they pounded across the parking lot toward them.

"Tess Showalter, NWNN," she said, catching her breath.

"No comment," the C.O. said.

"We understand you were discussing the upcoming march and rally," Tess went on.

"Who told you about this meeting?" the C.O. demanded.

"I can't reveal my sources," she said, forcing herself not to glance at Darrell. "Can you confirm the meeting was about the march and rally sponsored by the True Believers and EAR-C?"

"No comment," the C.O. barked. He got in the car and slammed the door.

"Would *you* care to comment, sir?" Tess said, turning to Darrell at last.

His expression was unreadable, but his response was crystal-clear: "No." He got in the car.

Tess watched the Navy men drive away. "He couldn't very well say anything to us in front of his boss," she said to Schuyler, somewhat defensively.

"I know that," Schuyler said in mild surprise. "*You* weren't expecting him to dish, were you?" He gestured toward the hedge. "Let's go over by the bushes and wait for the rest of them."

Twenty minutes later, it was nearly dark, and no one else had emerged. Security lights over the doorway clicked on against the gathering night. "Maybe they went out a different door," Tess ventured.

"Heather's car is here," Schuyler pointed out.

"But not the senators' car," she argued. "And not the last guy's. They could have gotten picked up on the other side of the building already."

"There's not enough room on that side to turn around," he said reasonably. "They'd either have to circle the church to get back on the road, or back out into traffic, which would be a bad idea on Prince William Parkway."

She blew out a breath. "I just hate waiting."

"I couldn't tell." He grinned at her.

"I always feel like I'm missing something." She crossed her arms and looked away from him.

"You are," he said, shrugging. "A decent dinner, a little relaxation time, some cuddling with that fine hunk of manflesh you're living with...."

She rounded on him. "We're just housemates!"

"Uh-huh." When she continued to glare at him, he pushed at the air in front of him. "Hey, don't get sore. I was just kidding around."

"Yeah, well, don't."

"Ah," he said sagely. "So you'd like to be cuddling with him, but it's not happening."

Savagely, Tess shoved away the memory of how it felt to be in Darrell's arms. "Just drop it, okay?"

"Okay. Fine."

"Good."

Silence reigned for a few moments. Then Schuyler said, "So how about those Nats?"

The door opened. Heather and Harkness walked out.

"Excuse me!" Tess said loudly. "Reverend Harkness!"

Heather glanced in her direction, grabbed Harkness's arm, and nearly dragged him to the car.

Undaunted, Tess shouted questions after the couple. "What were you discussing inside? What are the plans for the march? How many people do you expect will show up? Why are you calling in the military to help with security?"

The pair stopped dead. They exchanged a look. And then Heather, a sly smile on her face, turned around and approached Tess. "Is that thing on?" she demanded, pointing at the camera. At Tess's nod, she composed her face into a look of grave concern. "We're asking the military for protection because we expect to be attacked. The Indians will be massing at the National American

Indian Museum as we march by. They may be calling it a festival, but we're not fooled. And we intend to be prepared. Thank you." She wheeled away. Then, half-turning back, she added, "Put *that* in your peace pipe and smoke it." She got in the driver's seat as Harkness fumbled with the passenger side door. A moment more and he was in. Heather backed up and, with tires screaming, peeled out of the parking lot.

Tess shared a glance with Schuyler; he looked as shocked as she felt.

The black SUV pulled in as the door behind them opened again. Tess sloughed off her stupor and went back into action. "Senator! Senator Dickens!"

"No comment, young lady," Dickens said, smiling insincerely as he brushed past her to get to the car.

"Secretary Magnon, any comments on the meeting?" she persisted. The Defense Secretary glanced her way, but strode past her without a word.

"Senator Tyler!"

Tyler looked as if he were in over his head. He waved half-heartedly at the camera and ducked into the vehicle.

"Try Dickens again," Schuyler murmured, fiddling with the camera light. "I need a better shot of him." Tess nodded and they hurried to the SUV as Dickens was about to shut the door.

"Senator," Tess said, sticking her microphone into the gap, "Heather Willis says you're expecting Native Americans to attack your marchers. Is it true?"

Dickens' fake smile was still in place. "Did she, now?" He turned to the driver. "Let's go." And he slammed the door, nearly clipping Tess's arm.

The black SUV pulled out just as the mystery man's driver pulled in; as if choreographed, the man sailed past Tess and Schuyler to the car. "Sir!" Tess called to him. "Tess Showalter, NWNN."

He looked her up and down with eyes the color of whetted steel. "Nice to meet you," he said. In a fluid motion, he slipped into the car; the driver circled the lot and sped away.

Tess sighed. "Well, we got Heather's statement, anyway."

"Want to wait for Schulte?"

She shook her head. "I think he's small potatoes. But let's ask Tracie before we take off."

Tracie concurred. Schuyler loaded the camera into the back of the SUV and they took off for home.

"I didn't really expect you to get statements from anyone," Tracie said, when Tess and Schuyler had recounted their less-than-stellar results. "But we've got shots of all the players now, which is more than we had before."

"Indeed we do," Schuyler said with a fierce grin.

"And Heather gave us something, which surprised me," Tess said. "I didn't think she'd ever talk to us again."

"What Heather gave us was a lit stick of dynamite," Tracie said. "I wonder what she's up to."

"I wonder what Dickens is up to," Tess said. "Slimy bastard. And that mystery guy gives me the creeps."

"You said it," Schuyler agreed, glancing at her in the rear view mirror.

Tess was silent for a moment. "I'll talk to Darrell when I get home," she said. "See what I can get out of him off the record."

"Sounds good," Tracie said.

Schuyler glanced at the rear-view mirror again and shot her a knowing grin. Tess crossed her arms and ignored him.

Darrell felt as if his head housed a rock tumbler. Hard truths bounced against one another, caroming off the walls of his skull, inflicting pain with every strike.

He was a SEAL. An officer. He had to obey orders or be charged with insubordination.

His relations would be at the festival.

Court-martial would mean an end to his Navy career.

Nanabush needed him in the Navy.

His relations would be celebrating the Earth. They had no part in this.

If ordered, he would have to strike against his friends.

He could not hurt his friends. They had no part in this.

He was an officer. A leader.

His cousin would be there, and who knows how many others he had grown up with.

He was a warrior.

He was a healer.

He had to follow orders.

His relations had asked for his blessing.

He had to set an example for his men.

His relations trusted him to do the right thing.

"Shit," Paulsen muttered, interrupting the cacophony of his thoughts.

Darrell looked around. They were nearly to the Potomac; he could see, across the river, the upthrust point of the Washington Monument and the soaring roof of the Institute for Peace. "Sir?" he said.

"It won't work," he said. "We can't get our boats in there. The draft for the Tidal Basin inlet isn't deep enough."

Unfortunately for Darrell, his tactical ability had already solved that problem. "Kayaks, sir," he said, trying to keep the misery out of his voice. "We could use kayaks for the water approach."

The C.O. glanced over at him and grunted. "I'll pretend I didn't hear that."

"Sir?"

"I'm trying to get us out of this."

Ah. His heart lifted. "On second thought, sir, kayaks would be impractical for a number of reasons."

Paulsen shot him a twisted grin. "That's better."

The rock tumbler had slowed, but it hadn't stopped. Paulsen didn't want to do this any more than Darrell did. But that might not matter. After a moment, he said, "Sir, what if they don't buy it?"

"Then we'll have to get creative." He glanced again at Darrell as he made the turnoff for the Pentagon. "There's more than one way to follow orders."

As they got out of the car, Darrell said, "Sir, there's one thing you should know."

Paulsen paused with the car door open.

"I'm Potawatomi Indian."

"Yeah, I know. I reviewed your record when you came aboard." The C.O. glanced away for a moment. "I suppose you'll have friends at this thing."

"My cousin's coming from Michigan with our band's dance troupe. They're supposed to perform." His throat closed.

Paulsen closed his eyes. "Shit," he said again. Then he put a hand on Darrell's shoulder. "Don't worry, Warren. I'll get you out of this."

"Thank you, sir," he said. But he knew better than to trust his C.O.'s words as a guarantee. When the gods were involved, anything could happen.

He would just have to get creative.

He had forgotten about Tess. She was waiting for him in the kitchen when he let himself in the back door.

"What's going on?" she said without preamble.

As if he needed another gantlet to run tonight. He sighed. "How long have you been waiting for me?"

"Schuyler just dropped me off," she said. "He's taking the truck back to the studio. What did they say in the meeting?"

"You people never stop, do you?" He walked past her and headed for the basement stairs.

"That's not fair!"

He turned and regarded her. "There's such a thing as confidentiality, you know," he said. "Secret clearance. Need-to-know basis. You've heard of those?"

"Yeah, well, I need to know!" she said. "The world needs to know. The Indians need to know!" She said the last as if she were playing a trump card.

He turned back to her. "What is it you think 'the Indians' need to know?" he asked mildly.

"That the protestors expect them to attack!"

His eyes narrowed. "If you already know that much, then why do you need me?" He began to descend.

"Come on, Darrell!" she said from the top of the stairs, frustration plain in her voice. "We're supposed to be a team!"

He ignored her and kept walking. He heard her clatter down the stairs after him and sighed as he opened the door to his space. "Come on in," he said in resignation. "You're going to, anyway."

She glared at him as she passed through the doorway. He shut the door behind them and stood, arms crossed, while she looked around. It occurred to him that this was the first time she had ever been in his place. It also occurred to him that his bed lay on the other side of the curtain, and that even in his irritation, he was attracted to her. For a moment, he almost reached out and touched her.

Then she turned, and his desire shriveled at the look on her face. "Well?" she demanded, crossing her arms in turn. Whether she was mirroring his posture consciously or not, Darrell couldn't tell.

"This is off the record," he warned. "I could be court martialed if anyone found out."

"I know that," she said, her impatience plain. "I have no intention of quoting you. What. Did. They. Say?"

He sighed and plopped into the rickety folding chair, his forearms on his thighs as if they were holding him upright. In a sense, they were; he wanted nothing more out of this day than to escape into sleep. "All right," he said. "Senator Dickens is driving this. He asked the Defense Secretary for a special-ops force and Magnon recommended the team I'm on, because a couple of us saw action in Syria."

"You were in Syria?" she said. Comprehension dawned on her face. "My God, you were at Al-Laqbah! Weren't you?"

"Yeah," he said, pushing thoughts of the massacre away. "Anyway. Dickens wants our unit to sail into the Tidal Basin, and then deploy on the ground to the museum."

"He expects you to sail a warship into the *Tidal Basin?*" she said. "That's crazy!"

"It also won't work. The draft in the inlet isn't deep enough." Seeing her bewildered look, he added, "A warship would run aground. But we could use smaller craft."

She sank onto the edge of his sofa. "My God," she said again, softly. Her gaze flicked to him. "Does the museum know about this?"

"I don't know."

"Are you gonna tell them?"

"*Someone* certainly needs to." He looked hard at her. "Maybe a journalist ought to give them a call."

"Oh, I will," she said. "You can count on that." He saw her thinking shift. "Who was the guy who showed up last? We've ID'd everyone but him."

Darrell shrugged. "He said his name was Quinn. That's all I know. He seemed to be one of Dickens' cronies."

She nodded. "Thanks. That helps. And we've got his car's license number, too. We'll track him down." She paused. Then, more softly, she asked. "So do you know anybody going to the festival?" *Were you going to go?* seemed implicit in her tone.

He rolled his head back and looked at the rafters above them. "My hometown dance troupe is supposed to perform. My cousin contacted me last week." His relations had asked for his blessing. They trusted him to do the right thing. At her gasp, he looked straight at her. "I told my C.O. about it. He's going to try to get me out of the mission."

"What if he can't?" She looked horrified. "Oh, Darrell. What if you have to go anyway?"

"Then I'll have to get creative," he said. Inside his head, the rock tumbler had started revolving again. "What about you?" he asked, in an attempt to slow it down. "I guess you'll have to be on the Mall that day, too, won't you? To get the story and all?" His words came out more harshly than he meant them to, and she winced. "Sorry. I didn't mean it the way it sounded."

"No, you're right," she said. She dropped her eyes. "I'll be there." She laughed without humor. "I have to be."

Darrell heard anguish in her tone, and knew it wasn't just journalistic devotion driving her need. Morrigan wanted her there, too.

Gently, he said, "It works better if you don't fight Them." *Too often.*

She sighed and looked away.

At least her claws were sheathed. He took it as a sign to go on. "What scares you so much?" *What the hell happened between you and Her, anyway?*

Staring at the floor, Tess said, "We lost our farm to MegaAgriCorp."

He frowned at her *non sequitur.* "They bought you out?"

"No. My dad refused to sell. So they sued us for copyright infringement and a bunch of other bullshit." Her voice was bitter. "My parents settled, but part of the deal was that they couldn't ever say anything about it. Not only the terms of the agreement, but they could never mention MegaAgriCorp to anyone, ever again."

He nodded. "I've heard of that. The people who violated the prohibition were reduced to poverty."

"Yeah, well, that might have been better in the long run," she said. "The deal basically put us out of business. It broke Dad. A few years later, he tried to kill himself."

"Oh, God." He stifled an urge to hold her. Instead, he asked, "But how is Morrigan involved?"

Finally, she looked up at him. "She gave me an opportunity to get back at MegaAgriCorp. It was like, 'Just say the word and I will smite them for you.'" Her face twisted. "Or my dad. She would have made his life worse, too, if I'd told her to." She looked away again. "I was so angry with him that day. The agreement didn't include *me*, I was just a kid. But Dad told me I couldn't say anything, either."

"He was scared," Darrell said. "He didn't want you to get hurt. He loved you."

She laughed bitterly. "Yeah. He loved me and Mom so much that he wanted to leave us forever."

In a moment, she looked back at him. "Anyway, I couldn't do it. I ran away from Morrigan and Her offer. I couldn't bear to harm anyone. Not even the bastards who deserved it." Nearly whispering, she added, "I've been running from Her ever since."

"Kindness isn't a failing," he said.

"Oh, I am not kind," she said, her eyes hardening. "Don't believe that for a minute. I got into journalism because it allows me to uncover the truth, and the truth isn't kind."

"But it also sidelines you," he said, remembering her standing in the church parking lot, burning to know what had happened inside. "All you're doing is telling people about the hard choices others make. You don't have to make any of your own."

"Yeah, well," she said. "Maybe it's better this way." She stood. He knew she was on the verge of running. Again.

He got up, stepping between her and the door. "It's not," he said. "It's never better. Even refusing to choose is a choice."

"I have to go," she said.

"Tess..."

"Get out of my way, Darrell." Her eyes flashed in anger.

"Running won't solve this."

She put her hands on his chest and tried to push him out of the way. "Let me go!"

He wrapped his arms around her and kissed her.

He felt her respond. Then she pushed him away. For a moment, she stood in indecision, looking at the door with anguish written plainly on her face. But with tears in her eyes, she wrapped her arms around his neck and pulled his mouth to hers.

"I can't," he heard her murmur. "I can't." But she clung to him as if he could save her. And when he led her through the curtain and began to undress her, she didn't protest.

Chapter 12

Harkness groped for the phone, knocking it off the nightstand. It hit the thick carpet and kept ringing. Groaning, he glanced at the time on the bedside clock – 5:45 a.m.

He rolled out of bed to retrieve the phone. "Hello?"

"Who has that girl been talking to?"

Harkness blinked sleep out of his eyes and glanced at the bed. Heather was awake and facing him; he saw the clock's blue glow reflected in her eyes. He smiled at her and headed for the living room, closing the bedroom door behind him.

"What do you mean, Senator?" he said, when he judged he was far enough away to have a private conversation.

"You know what I mean. That reporter outside the meeting last night. How did she know to be there?"

"I don't know," Harkness said honestly. "Heather talked to her one day last week, but as far as I know, she hasn't talked to her since."

"I need information on her."

"On Heather?" Harkness blinked.

"No, you dolt! On the reporter! Let me talk to the girl."

Call me a dolt, will you? The fingers of his free hand curled into a fist. "Can it wait?" he said brusquely. "She's still asleep." He glanced toward the bedroom door. It opened, giving him a vision of her in a dressing gown. As she tied it, the V-neckline gapped, giving him a view of one delicious breast. He swallowed.

"Wake her up, then!"

Harkness unclenched his fist as she approached him. "It's Dickens," he whispered. "He wants to talk to you." He handed the phone over, brushing the bare skin between her breasts suggestively. She batted his hand away; apparently thinking better of it, she grabbed his hand and directed it to her breast as she gave him a lingering kiss.

Then she moved away from him. *God forgive me, but she is something else.* "Hello, Senator," she said huskily into the phone. "What can I do for you?" He watched her hungrily as she perched on the arm of the rental sofa, staring out at the lightening sky to the east. "Yes, I've spoken with her. ... No, of course not! I wouldn't have told her that! ... Her name's Tess Showalter. I thought at first she worked for Channel 10. ... Because an old friend introduced us. ... Sue Killeen. We palled around together in high school. I hadn't spoken to her in years before she.... Well, I guess they met in college. That's what the reporter told me when.... Oh, you have my word, Senator. I have no intention of ever speaking to Tess Showalter again." She held the phone out to him. "He wants to talk to you again."

Sighing, Harkness took the device. "Yes, Senator," he said, as Heather ran the backs of her fingers down his chest.

"Are your people in place?"

"Yes, of course," he lied. He had a few more calls to make, some numbers to solidify. But the buses were rented and the overnight accommodations had been secured — Heather had seen to all of that.

"And your numbers are solid? You promised me a big turnout, Harkness — tens of thousands of people. Are you sure you can deliver?"

Heather had slipped her hand below the waistband of his boxers. "Oh, I'll deliver," he said, his voice deeper than he meant it to be.

Dickens sighed loudly. "Just don't fuck this up. Or you'll wish Hell was real." He ended the call.

Heather's mouth was following the same route her hand had taken. Harkness dropped the phone; it landed soundlessly on the carpet.

Tess awoke in her own bed. She glanced at her phone and panicked, thinking she had overslept. Then she remembered it was Saturday. She wasn't supposed to meet Tracie and Schuyler to go over their game plan until after noon.

Tracie and Schuyler. The meeting last night. The confrontation with Darrell — and what came afterward.

She groaned and rolled over, acknowledging the ache in her groin and cursing herself for it. *What the hell was I thinking?*

Yes, of course, she was attracted to him. But did she have to act on it? This was going to complicate everything — with Darrell, with Sue, with the story she was working on. She'd compromised herself with a source. And Sue was going to be hurt when she found out.

If she found out. Did she need to know?

Not if it didn't happen again.

God knows she had kept enough of her college trysts from Sue for the very same reason.

She sighed. *I need to move out.* The thought had occurred to her periodically over the years. Her relationship with Sue had been going downhill even before Ginger left. But until now, she hadn't been making enough money to afford a decent apartment on her own. Now that she was at the network, however, she might even be able to buy a condo.

Of course, that meant keeping her job. And *that* meant no more sleeping with sources.

Resolved, she closed her eyes. Then they flew open again. Who was she kidding? She had *needed* Darrell last night. She'd confessed her weakness to him, and still he had made love to her. His touch was like a benediction. Like redemption.

She was going to have a hard time giving that up.

"You don't have to," Morrigan purred in her ear.

She shot upright, trembling. She looked around wildly, but the goddess had not manifested. Still shaking, she lay back down again, huddling into a ball, willing Morrigan to go away.

It didn't work. It never worked with Her. "He can be yours forever," the goddess whispered.

"I can't," Tess mumbled.

"You can," the goddess said. "All you have to do is choose."

Sue squinted at the light angling through the dining room window and reached for her coffee mug. She raised it to her lips and was surprised to find it empty. *When did I finish that last cup?*

She had been up for hours, finalizing details for the Earth Power Week show. She rubbed her eyes and was about to get up for more coffee when Tess finally made an appearance. "Good morning, sleepyhead," she said. "Coffee's ready."

"No, it's not." Tess dumped the old grounds and rinsed the pot.

Sue grimaced. "Guess I drank more this morning than I thought."

"It's okay." Tess loaded the machine and hit the start button.

In a moment, the scent of fresh coffee reached Sue, making her smile. "Thanks."

"Sure."

"You got in late last night."

"Yeah, and I have to work this afternoon," Tess said. "We need to air our story this week."

"Want another angle?" Sue asked. "That's what you call it, right? An angle?"

Tess glanced at her through the pass-through, the corners of her mouth turned up. "Depends on what you're talking about."

"I had a meeting with the people in my group last night," Sue said. "We're planning a massive ritual of protection on the Mall next Saturday."

"Oh?"

"Yeah. Several Pagan groups are going to help us. We intend to bless the Mall from the Washington Monument grounds all the way to the Capitol."

Tess leaned back against the sink. "That's gonna take a lot of people."

Sue nodded, feeling smug. "We've got definite commitments from five hundred. We all want to show our solidarity with the Native Americans."

Tess was regarding her strangely. Finally she said, "I don't know if that's a good idea."

"Why not?"

"Because we have reason to believe that the military's going to be called out," she said carefully.

Sue blinked. "To protect the Indians?"

"No. To protect the marchers." Tess made air quotes around the word *protect.*

"From the Indians?" Sue was incredulous. "That's crazy! When did you find this out?"

"Last night."

"Does Darrell know about this?"

Tess turned her back to Sue and reached into the cabinet for a mug. "He's the one who told me."

"Do the Indians know?"

Tess shook her head. "I don't think so. I need to call the museum on Monday."

"That's not going to be enough time," Sue said, shutting down her laptop. "I've got to go down there anyway today to check on our setup. I'll swing by the museum while I'm there."

"Oh, right!" Tess said as she turned to the stove. "How's your event coming?"

Sue thought she seemed relieved to talk about something else, which struck her as a little odd. But as the new topic was Earth Power Week, she was more than willing to oblige. "It's going to be wonderful. We've got a wind farm set up on the Mall."

"No kidding? But those turbines are huge, aren't they?"

"The regular ones are. Ours are only half size. But between them and the solar panels, we'll generate enough power for the whole show."

"Cool," Tess said. "Maybe we can do a story on it this week."

"Sounds great," Sue said with a grin.

"So," Tess said, stirring her eggs, "have you seen Darrell today?"

"Nope. And I've been up since six. Either he left really early or he's still downstairs. Why?"

Tess shrugged. "Just wondered, that's all."

Suspicion darkened the bright morning. Sue studied her roommate for a moment. No, Tess didn't appear to be hiding anything. And she had come down from her own bedroom, not up from the basement.

Tess looked up from the stove. "What?" she challenged.

"Nothing," Sue said. She grabbed her purse and headed through the kitchen to the back door. "See you later."

Everything on the Mall appeared to be in good order. Sue checked the mounts for the wind turbines and the locks on the portable solar generators. The solar panels were already soaking up the sun, but the seven horizontal-axis turbines wouldn't be turned on until a test run Sunday. Then they'd be fired up early Monday morning and would run all week.

Even at half-height, the windmills were impressive. Lined up in the middle of the Mall from 14th Street Northwest to the Capitol grounds, they dwarfed the Smithsonian buildings on either side and, from certain angles, looked taller than the Washington Monument. Sue was proud of her ingenuity in getting the manufacturer to arrange the display. She half-hoped the Park Service would agree to buy the turbines and make them a permanent fixture on the Mall.

She checked in at all the tents along the way, finally arriving at the off-the-grid demonstration house just north of the National Museum of the American Indian. The builders were on site, putting the finishing touches to the house, and invited her to tour the interior. She agreed that the house had all the common comforts and would be a terrific deal for some lucky person. EiB planned to raffle off the house, relocation costs and all, as part of the show.

Thanking her tour guides, she struck out for the American Indian museum.

She knew a lot of people didn't understand the museum, even after nearly twenty years of operation. Visitors tended to expect a bunch of static exhibits of teepees and buffaloes. What they got instead, if they stuck around and gave the place a chance, was an immersion into the Native cultures that still existed throughout the Americas – cultures that had flourished anew since the Second Coming ten years before. Their gods had seen to it that proper attention was finally being paid to Their people. Great strides had been made to alleviate the squalor on Native reservations, and to provide reparations for the treaties that had been systematically violated over the years. It was costing the government billions of dollars, but funds had become available for it, as well as for other long-neglected humanitarian projects, as the great military-industrial complex had begun winding down.

The museum, as a concrete symbol of this sea change, had been attacked several times. Vandals had smashed windows, ripped display panels from the walls, and painted epithets on the grandfather rocks and the boulders that marked the cardinal directions outside. But all of those attacks had occurred under cover of darkness. So far, the Indians themselves had not been attacked at the museum – although one couldn't say the same about their brethren elsewhere in the country.

Sue could never understand how people who professed to be filled with God's love could be so full of hatred for such a beautiful building. It was her favorite museum on the Mall. Every time she entered it, she felt as if she were passing into sacred space.

Although she had to admit that the security guards checking backpacks and purses at the door kind of killed the mood.

She approached the visitor's desk and inquired whether any of the managers were in. She was in luck: the public affairs director was putting the finishing touches on materials for next week's festival. Sue waited for a few minutes in the atrium, watching children flit across the compass rose set into the floor, until a guard came to show her to the public affairs office.

The woman who met Sue was pleasant enough. She listened to her politely, expressed concern for the danger the festival was in, expressed thanks for the invitation to participate in the Pagan blessing of the Mall Saturday morning, and promised to pass it along.

Sue got the distinct impression that the woman hadn't taken her seriously. Disheartened, she caught the next Blue Line train home.

A tantalizing aroma greeted her when she walked in the front door. Darrell was presiding over several pots on the stove. "Perfect timing," he said with a grin. "Dinner's almost ready. Want some?"

"How could I turn it down? It smells divine," she said. "What are you making?"

"Salmon and wild rice," he said. "I saw a box of wild rice at the grocery store and it reminded me of home."

"Do you miss it?" she said as she set the table for the two of them.

He shrugged. "Some days more than others. Today, it wasn't bad until I saw the rice."

As they sat down, Sue said, "I'm glad I caught you," and went on to describe her meeting with the public affairs director at the NMAI.

He put his fork down and shook his head. "I'm not surprised, really. She's not high enough up the food chain. Plus as soon as you said you were Pagan, she probably decided you were a nut."

"But I didn't even wear my Earth shoes," she said in mock protest.

He smiled. "Thanks for trying, anyway. I plan to call my cousin to warn him."

"Good," Sue said, relieved. "If you talk to him again, please let him know we would love to have him and the other dancers at the ritual Saturday morning."

"I'll tell him," Darrell promised.

The back door opened, admitting a tired-looking Tess. "Oh, man," she said, "did I miss dinner? I even brought the booze." She held up two bottles of wine.

"There's plenty left," Darrell said, springing out of his chair. He approached Tess, leaning toward her as she put the bottle on the kitchen counter. She shook her head slightly and nodded toward Sue; he glanced back at her and moved away from Tess. Then he said something else, but Sue stopped listening. Her dinner began digging a hole in the pit of her stomach.

"Sue?" Darrell was standing by her elbow.

She looked up at him. "Huh?"

"I said, 'Tell Tess what you told me about the museum,'" he said. "Are you okay?"

"No," she said. "No. All of a sudden, I don't feel well. I think I'll go upstairs and lie down."

Somehow, she made it upstairs and got into bed, fully dressed, all while the litany of the past ten years played over and over in her head. *It's never me. It's always Tess. Never me. She gets all the guys and she doesn't care. I never win.*

She cried silently, muffling her sobs in her pillow. She didn't want Tess to know she'd won.

Tess threw up her hands. "She didn't even feed the cats."

"I did it while I was making dinner," Darrell said. "Should I go after her?" He cast an anxious glance at the stairs.

"No, she'll be fine," Tess said in disgust, sitting down with her plate in the chair Sue had just vacated and scooting Sue's plate out of the way. "She just needs to cry it out."

Darrell opened one of the bottles of wine and poured two glasses. He set one before Tess and sprawled in the other chair, sipping his glass and studying her.

"What?" Tess said, glancing up from her food.

"This happens a lot, I take it."

"Pretty frequently. Not so much since we got out of college. We don't really run in the same circles any more." Tess took another bite. "This is really good. Did you make it?"

"Yeah." He swirled the wine in his glass. "I'm not a great cook, but I know how to make salmon." He took another sip and sat up, leaning his forearms on the table. "Does it bother you?"

"That you can cook?"

"That Sue gets upset every time you get in a relationship."

She paused, fork in hand. "Are we 'in a relationship'?"

"You know what I mean."

She swallowed a mouthful of wine before answering. "It used to. Now I'm just tired of it." She put her fork down and pushed her plate away. "Sue's always had issues with self-esteem. She was always heavier than the other girls in her class – or thought she was." Tess snorted a laugh. "Maybe she really was. I mean, you've seen Heather.

"Anyway, Sue's mom is one of these women who are obsessed with being thin, and she was always on Sue to lose weight. She was bulimic for a while when we were in college."

"My God," he said.

"Yeah, it was pretty hairy. But she got a handle on it and we all thought she'd be okay. And then this crap started. 'I'll never get a man. I'm too fat. They all like you better.' The guys would pick up on her desperation and run away screaming. Sometimes they'd run to me." She shrugged. "But I wasn't really into any of them. I guess some of them would go to Sue then and ask her how to get me to like them."

"Not the most comfortable position for her to be in." He finished his glass and poured himself another, then topped off hers and went for the second bottle. "Didn't it bother you?" he asked from the kitchen.

"Well, yeah. I mean, it did for a while." She pushed away her plate and studied the wine in her glass. "Like I said, it got old. I couldn't go out with anybody without her saying she was interested in him and I was supposedly taking him away from her."

"So you quit going out."

"Well." She took a long drink. "I had my career to consider, too."

He regarded her, eyebrows raised.

"I don't like to date people I work with," she elaborated. "It gets too complicated. And with the crazy hours I work, there's not much chance to meet anybody else." She looked up at him. "What is this, Analyze Tess Day? What about you?"

He shrugged. "What *about* me?"

"Anything I should know about your dating history?"

"I'm divorced." He watched her over the rim of his glass.

"Really," she said. "How long ago?"

"A couple of years." Now it was his turn to study the wine in his glass. "She couldn't hack being a Navy wife, so she moved back home." He sounded wistful.

"Dated anybody since then?" she asked.

"No." He sat back again. "Not 'til now."

They were silent for a few moments: she went back to gazing at her glass; he went back to studying her. Finally she looked up. "What?" she said, a slow smile lighting her lips.

He leaned forward and kissed her.

That night, she never made it up to her own bed.

Darrell was making coffee when Sue came down the stairs the next morning. When she saw him, she nearly turned around and went back up. Or left through the front door without eating. Anything to avoid seeing him. Anything to avoid being with him.

But he'd seen her. "Sue," he said. "There you are. Come and have coffee with me."

"I'm late," she said, inching toward the front door. "I need to get down to the Mall."

"Bullshit," he said. "Come and sit with me."

"Wouldn't you rather have Tess join you?" The bitter words slipped out before she could catch herself. She had just passed Tess's bedroom, and its wide-open door and empty bed had given her a pretty good idea of where Tess had spent the night.

Darrell filled a fresh mug with coffee from the pot. He crossed into the living room and held the mug out to her. "Come and sit with me," he said again.

She sighed in defeat and took the mug.

"Now," he said as he joined her at the table with his own mug, "what is the deal with you two?"

"Why do you care?" The coffee scalded her throat.

He regarded her with a serious expression. "We're supposed to be a team."

"Well, you should have thought of that before you fucked one of us." She stood. "I need to go."

"Sit down," he barked. Her eyes flew open in surprise, but she sat.

"Tess says you always do this," he said.

"What?"

"Play the victim."

Her mouth dropped open. "How dare you —"

"And as far as I can see," he went on relentlessly, "she's right. You would rather complain about Tess taking all the men than go out and find one for yourself." He leaned forward. "The two of you have completely different lives, Sue. The only thing I can see that you share right now is this house. Why are you blaming her for your lack of a relationship?"

"Because she's cute," Sue said, unable to stem the scorn dripping from each syllable. "She's petite, and she's perky, and she's on TV. Every guy who meets her is drawn to her like a moth to a flame." She ducked her head. "I can't compete with her."

"Then find someone who's never met her," he said. "Stop allowing yourself to settle for sloppy seconds." He smiled a little. "There's no reason for it. You're a beautiful woman, Sue. Some guys prefer tall women. Some prefer women with...."

"If you say 'with meat on their bones,' I will slug you," she said hoarsely.

"I was going to say 'with brains,'" he said. "Because you're also intelligent. And you've got organizational skills out the wazoo. My God, woman, you're putting together a week-long show on the National Mall, it's the morning before opening day, and you're not a frazzled mess. Do you know how many people could do that?"

"Lots," she said.

He shook his head. "Hardly anyone. I'd be over in the corner, rocking myself and sucking my thumb."

She snorted and looked down at her coffee.

"Look," he went on. "I have no idea where this thing with Tess is going. She doesn't, either. And really, it shouldn't matter. The three of us have got a job to do, and we need to put aside whatever our personal issues are and just get the job done."

She nodded and rose. She dumped the rest of her coffee into the sink and rinsed the mug. Then, still silent, she headed for the back door.

"You need to clear the air with Tess," he said as she turned the handle.

She looked back, careful to keep a neutral expression on her face. "Later. After the show is over." And she shut the door behind her.

Chapter 13

"Got him," Tracie said with satisfaction.

Tess practically ran over to her computer. "You found the elusive Quinn? Really?" She looked over her shoulder at the screen. "Oh, my God."

"Well? Who is he?" Schuyler asked, leaning back in his chair. He had taken to hanging out with Tess and Tracie when he had a few minutes to spare.

"Malcolm Quinn is the president and chief executive officer of Integrated Deterrence Systems Incorporated," Tracie read aloud. She punched in another search. "Defense contractor. Headquartered in McLean. Does huge bank with Homeland Security, too."

"Big surprise," Schuyler said. "So what was he doing at the meeting?"

"Well, that's obvious, isn't it?" Tess said. "When the defense budget was cut, his company lost income. Probably a lot of income."

"Sure," Tracie said. "But why is he getting involved with the planning for this march? What's in it for him?"

"People see pictures of the military opening fire on Native Americans and they get scared," Schuyler said. "So they yell for Congress to give more money to the military to put down the Indians, and so they do. Right? More money for Quinn."

"But it wouldn't take long to bring down the Native Americans," Tracie said. "There aren't that many of them, and they don't have the same level of defense technology that the military does."

"It'd be a cakewalk," Tess said, her mouth suddenly dry.

"Right," Tracie said. "And then what? Who do they go after then? Because we've gotta keep that military spending high." She shook her head. "There's something we're missing."

"Let's go talk to Antonia," Tess said.

Together, they trooped down to Antonia's office.

She welcomed them. "I was just about to come and see you anyway," she said. "The march is Saturday. We need to air something this week."

"We know," Tracie said. "And we think we've got enough to go with, but we might be missing the bigger picture."

"Let's hear what you've got." Antonia sat back while Tess and Tracie tag-teamed their explanation of what they had found.

"Wait," Antonia said, holding up her hand, when they had told her about the result of Tess's first interview with Heather. "Are you telling me that the source told you not to air the interview?"

"Well, yeah," Tess said, exchanging a look with Schuyler.

"We can't use it on the air, then. It would be unethical."

Tess was about to argue, but Tracie stepped in. "It doesn't matter. We got better tape from her after the planning meeting, anyway."

"Let's see it," Antonia said. So Tess opened her tablet and showed the raw footage to their boss. Antonia sucked in a breath on the last line. "It's great tape," she said. "But I wonder why she's telling us this." She tapped her upper lip with a forefinger. "Give me the list of the people who were at this meeting."

"Heather Willis, obviously," Tracie said as Antonia typed the names into her computer. "She came with Milton Harkness."

Antonia's head snapped up. "Harkness? The guy who kidnapped Naomi Curtis?"

"Yep. The same guy."

"So he's out of prison, huh? Interesting." She typed Harkness's name into her list. "Who else was there?"

Tracie reeled off the names of the senators and the Defense Secretary – none of which seemed to surprise Antonia – and of the Navy men. Tess explained Dickens had specifically asked for their unit because they had seen action at Al-Laqbah. Antonia shook her head over that.

"And this guy," Tracie said. "Malcolm Quinn." She handed over her tablet so Antonia could see his picture and bio.

"I've heard of him," Antonia said, looking over the information on the screen. "Former Marine. Supposedly founded Integrated Deterrence Systems with money he inherited from a rich uncle, but no record of the uncle's existence was ever found."

"Where'd he get the money from, then?" Schuyler asked.

"Spying, according to the rumors," Antonia said. "But the CIA supposedly hasn't been able to pin anything definite on him. Anyway, he's gotten rich from selling arms to both sides in various conflicts around the world. Usually with the blessing of the United

States, but sometimes without it. And we buy from him, too – DoD is a big customer, and so is Homeland Security." She handed the tablet back to Tracie. "Is that it?"

"Just Reverend Schulte," Tess said. "But we think he was involved because the meeting was at his church."

"And Harkness needed somebody else on his side," Antonia said. "Okay. So tell me if I'm understanding this right: the True Believers and EAR-C plan to provoke a fight with a bunch of unarmed Indians, and then the heroes of Al-Laqbah are supposed to swoop in from the Tidal Basin and detain the Indians as a threat to national security and the American way of life. Is that about it?"

"That sums it up nicely, yes," said Tracie. "Which keeps the military in business just long enough to put down the supposed Indian uprising, so we can go back to business as usual – or rather, business as it was before the Second Coming. But then what?"

Antonia shrugged. "Then they stage another crisis, so they can keep the money flowing to the military-industrial complex."

"But..." Tracie began.

"They're really good at this," Antonia told her. "They've had years and years of practice."

"And in the meantime," Tess said darkly, "people die." Her gut clenched at the thought of Darrell's friends being at the museum on Saturday. "We've got to expose them."

"Pull it together for today's show," Antonia said. "That will give us all week to gather reaction. We can run follow-ups every day until the big event on Saturday." She stood, grinning. "Great work, guys. Now go write me a Pulitzer Prize winner."

With some trepidation, Darrell approached the C.O.'s office. He could think of only one reason why Paulsen would want to see him this morning, and he was pretty sure he wasn't going to like what the man had to say.

He was right. "Shut the door, Warren," Paulsen said after returning Darrell's salute. As soon as the door was closed, the C.O. let out an explosive sigh. "Have a seat."

"It's bad news, isn't it, sir?"

"I just got off the phone with the Secretary of the Navy," he began.

Darrell blinked in surprise. *He went all the way up the chain of command to the SecNav?*

"And it's a no go," Paulsen went on. "We are definitely going to have to perform in Senator Dickens' dog-and-pony show on Saturday. The only way any of us can get out of it is by being dead. Or by being so close to dead as to be indistinguishable from it." The corners of his mouth lifted briefly. "I'm sorry, Darrell. I did my best to get you out of this." His eyes lost focus. "I did my best to get us *all* out of this. It's a fool's errand, and I'm afraid we're going to be the ones looking like fools."

"Thank you for trying, sir," Darrell said.

Paulsen remained silent, lost in thought.

"Sir, is that all?" Darrell asked quietly.

The C.O. came back to himself with a start. "Yes. Dismissed."

Darrell stood and saluted; Paulsen stood and returned the salute. "Shut the door behind you, son," Paulsen said as Darrell let himself out.

He let his shoulders slump a little as he walked away from the C.O.'s office. He had known what the answer would be; why was he feeling so defeated?

Back at his desk, he opened his browser. *Bozho, Mike,* he typed in the instant message box. *Got your ears on?*

Bozho! Ni je na? came the immediate answer. Darrell smiled. *Anwe she shena. What are you up to?*

Packing. I hear it will be hot in D.C. this weekend.

Darrell laughed quietly and typed, *It's August! Of course it will be hot in D.C. But the museum is air conditioned.*

That will be a blessing, his cousin typed back. *I will let the dancers know.*

Darrell's smile faded as he typed the next line. *I need to warn you about something, cuz. I've heard there's going to be a big march and rally on Saturday. EAR-C is involved.*

Oh? That's not good.

No, it's not good at all. Darrell paused, weighing how to phrase the next part. Finally, he typed, *It's likely there will be some trouble.*

His cousin's pause was longer. *Do we need to bring warriors as well as dancers?*

Darrell closed his eyes for a moment. *I will leave that up to you. Listen, the local Pagans are planning a protective ritual on the Mall Saturday morning. You're all invited to take part.*

Good to know. I'll tell the others. Another long pause. *I should warn you of something, too, cuz. Ruthie is coming down with us.*

Darrell went cold. *Why?* his fingers typed, unbidden.

You'll have to ask her yourself, came the reply. *See you Friday night.*

Bama mine, Darrell typed. Then he closed the browser and went into the bathroom. He went into a stall, closed the door, and leaned against the wall. His eyes looked in the direction of the ceiling but saw nothing.

Nothing but Ruthie as he'd seen her before his last deployment: her face streaked with tears as she clung to him, begging him not to go. "I have a bad feeling about this one," she kept saying. "Please don't leave me."

Nothing but the dismay on her face when he returned: "You're so different," she kept saying. "So...hard. Not the man I married. Where's my carefree husband? Where's the caring, patient, loving Darrell I used to know?" *I left him behind in Syria. He was a casualty of friendly fire, killed while trying to save a village full of civilians who didn't deserve to die.*

Nothing but the fear in her eyes when he exploded after finding out that she had begun gambling again while he was deployed. She had been blowing the money in Atlantic City that he had risked his life to earn.

Nothing but the expression she wore when he left for work that final morning: clear-eyed, calm and resigned. Her kiss was perfunctory. When he came home that night, she was gone.

He groaned. He had to see her again. He couldn't bear to see her again. He wanted her back. He wouldn't take her back if she begged him.

He had Tess now. Maybe. *Are we "in a relationship"?*

He would have to tell Tess that Ruthie was coming back.

And then he groaned again, louder, as the realization hit him: Ruthie was coming with the dancers. She would be at the museum Saturday when he gave his platoon the order to attack.

And there was nothing he could do about it.

It happened every year during Earth Power Week: Sue would leave home Sunday morning and devote every waking minute to the show until the final exhibit came down the following weekend. Her head was always full of logistical details: a speaker would be late or ill-prepared; the stovetop in the cooking tent would malfunction; or somebody would think the composting toilet in the demonstration house was actually hooked up and use it, despite about a million signs to the contrary. The previous year, it had happened twice. After the second incident, she had told the builders to nail down the lid.

This year, though, she had apparently done the show enough times – this was her fifth year of involvement and her third as project manager – that she could free up some brainpower for other things. Unfortunately, what her brain wanted to dwell on was the one-sided conversation she'd had with Darrell Sunday morning.

The more she thought about it, the angrier she became. How dare he accuse her of playing the victim? He had only known her and Tess for a few weeks. He didn't know how far back their acrimony went – how Tess had seemed to care about Sue's feelings at first, but then turned on her. She had even told Sue, not long ago, that she would see whomever she wanted to see, and she didn't need to ask Sue's permission first. As if that was what this was all about.

The jerk also didn't know what Sue had gone through, even before she had gotten to college: the awkwardness she had felt around Heather, a.k.a. Miss Perfect, and how much she had hated Heather bossing her and their friend Moira around. Moira didn't seem to mind; she was happy to be a follower, and she didn't much care who she was following. But it rankled Sue. She was smarter than Heather, but Heather had more charisma. She always attracted all the attention. Just like Tess.

Sue wondered briefly why she always got mixed up with women who hogged the limelight.

And speaking of hogging the limelight, of course Tess had to break her story on the first day of Sue's show. Her boss called her to tell her to find a monitor and watch the story, as it could have a bearing on the Earth Power Week exhibits. Sue sighed and made her way to the command trailer, where a couple of interns, taking a break in the air conditioning, were already watching the show.

Antonia Greco's face filled the screen. "Earlier in this broadcast, we told you about EAR-C and the Believers in the One True God – the groups planning a major march and rally on the National Mall here in Washington this coming Saturday. We now have word that two U.S. senators are involved in the planning for that event. Our investigative reporter, Tess Showalter, has the details. Tess?"

"Thanks, Antonia," her roommate said, as the camera switched to her pixie face. "TAaNA has learned Senators Russell Dickens of

Alabama and Adam Tyler of Illinois attended a recent planning meeting for the march – a meeting also attended by True Believers officials and members of the U.S. Navy. We spoke with Heather Willis of the True Believers after the meeting. She told us why the Navy was getting involved."

Now the shot changed to Heather's face. Sue thought she looked haggard, as though she hadn't been sleeping well. When Heather gave out that crazy story about how they expected the Indians to attack the marchers, Sue clucked her tongue and shook her head. One of the interns turned around and glared at her.

"What?" she said. "It's bullshit. If anybody's going to start trouble, it'll be those religious nutjobs, not the Indians. They'll be celebrating the Earth, the same as we are."

The young man barked a laugh. "They're just waiting for their chance to take over," he said. "They've always thought they owned this country. Ever since Jesus came back, they've been trying to get us whites to go back where we came from."

He said it so matter-of-factly that Sue, stunned, missed the rest of Tess's report. She finally focused again on the screen as Antonia said, "We'll have more on this story as it develops this week. Thanks, Tess. Next up on 'Talk About a New America'...."

"Okay, show's over," Sue said. "Back to work, you guys." The interns turned off the monitor and loped off. As soon as the door shut on them, she picked up the phone.

If her boss wanted to keep that anti-Native kid on staff until his internship was over, she could have him. But Sue wanted him off her project. She wasn't going to have any trash talk about Native Americans on her staff – even if Darrell *was* a jerk.

"Things are coming along nicely," Nanabush said. He had called up a chaise longue from somewhere and was reclining on it – to the consternation of Morrigan, who stood stiffly next to His aimlessly waving feet.

"Did You have to complicate things quite so much?" Gaia asked with a sigh.

"I can't help it that My human is such a stud," the rabbit-eared god replied. "Couldn't You two have picked humans who liked each other better?"

"They got along fine in the beginning," Gaia said, glancing at Morrigan, who shrugged eloquently. "But Nanabozho, really. Did You have to bring the ex-wife into it, too?"

He grinned rakishly. "Hey, I have no control over Ruthie. That's all on her. Anyway, I didn't think We were here to discuss the humans."

Morrigan regarded Him skeptically for a moment; He continued to smile engagingly at Her. Finally, with a gusty sigh, She said, "I want to know what Lucifer is up to."

Gaia gave a short laugh. "Don't We all."

Morrigan said, "He can't mean to just open fire on a group of unarmed civilians – it would be a public relations disaster. Their media would get hold of it and never let go. Public opinion would turn against him immediately." She frowned. "No, he must have another trick up his sleeve." She and Gaia both stared at Nanabush.

His eyes widened and his ears stood straight up. "What are you looking at *Me* for? I'm certainly not privy to Lucifer's counsel."

"But you're a Trickster," Gaia said. "You must know what he's thinking."

"I told You this wouldn't work," Morrigan said to Gaia. "He doesn't know what's going on in His own head half the time."

Nanabush hopped off the chaise and stood nose-to-nose with Her. "I beg Your pardon," He said. "I know what's going on in My own head at least three-quarters of the time."

Gaia laughed, earning a wink from Nanabush and a glare from Morrigan. "Really, Nanabush," She said. "I just thought You might have...hmm. Let's call it an educated guess. If You were Lucifer, how would You go about precipitating such an act of violence against the Indians?"

"I'd give the military a hot foot," He said instantly.

Morrigan rolled Her eyes. "He's been watching 'Bugs Bunny' again."

"Figuratively speaking," Nanabush went on, appearing to ignore Morrigan, although laughter danced in His eyes. "What I mean is, I would put in a ringer. Someone to fire the first shot."

"But someone who would blend into the crowd," Morrigan said thoughtfully. "Someone who wouldn't be noticed until the shooting started."

"It would probably have to be an Indian," Gaia mused.

"Who do We know who might fit that profile?" Morrigan asked.

After another moment, all three of Them looked at one another and said simultaneously: "Ruthie."

"Darrell," said Nanabush, "we need to talk."

"So talk," Darrell said as he checked out his reflection in the half-bath's mirror. He straightened the collar of his shirt.

"Where are you going, anyway?"

Darrell grinned at him. "I'm taking Tess out to dinner. Her story broke today – her first big one. Did you see it?" he asked the god.

"No," Nanabush said. "Since the advent of HDTV, I don't pick up much on these." He twitched his ears.

Darrell threw back his head and laughed. Nanabush regarded his reaction with some surprise. "It wasn't *that* funny," He said. "Things must be going really well between you and Tess."

"Pretty well," Darrell said with a jaunty smile. "And she was magnificent today."

"Oh, pshaw," the god said with a wave. "You're just taken with the idea that you're dating a woman who's seen in millions of homes every day."

Darrell waggled his eyebrows and picked up his hairbrush.

"I bet the guys at work were very impressed when you made them watch her report."

"Not only that," Darrell said, "but they all think she's hot. Which she is."

"Hmm," Nanabush said.

Darrell paused while brushing his hair to glance at Him. "What?"

"Well, I'm just kind of surprised at how quickly she's pushed any thought of Ruthie out of your head." The god said it carelessly, but He watched for Darrell's reaction.

Darrell turned to face Nanabush and said simply, "Maybe it's time. How do I look?"

"Stunning," the god said. "Listen, about Ruthie...."

Darrell turned to Nanabush. "Look, there's nothing to worry about. I doubt I'll even have time to talk to her." He ticked off dates on his fingers. "I will probably see her Friday night at the blessing ceremony, but I'll be pretty busy then. I'm not going to the performance on Saturday because I have to be part of Senator Dickens' dog-and-pony show. And the troupe goes home Sunday." He turned back to the mirror. "I don't get You, Nanabush. All these months, You've been pushing me to get over Ruthie, and now that I've done it, it's like You're trying to get me to reconsider."

Nanabush shook his head. "That's not it at all. I'm just wondering whether you thought she could ever be...." He waggled His eyebrows in turn. "Lured to the Dark Side."

"What?" Darrell gave Him an incredulous look. "No way. Not the Ruthie I knew."

"But what if she had gambling debts?" the god persisted.

Darrell frowned and cocked his head. Then the back door slammed and his expression cleared. "There's Tess. Do I look okay?"

"Stunning," the god said. "She won't be able to keep her hands off you."

"Maybe I should tone it down then, huh? We should at least have dinner first." He winked and opened the door, holding out his arms to Tess.

Nanabush sighed. "'Not the Ruthie *I* knew,'" he mimicked. "That's not what I asked you, Darrell, My boy."

Chapter 14

Rusty Dickens was not particularly smart. But then, brains were a drawback in politics. If you came off like an egghead, people wouldn't vote for you. They didn't like their politicians to be smarter than they were. It was okay to be folksy, but not smart. Belligerent was okay, too, as long as you got belligerent about the right things.

No, Dickens wasn't particularly smart. But he prided himself on his cunning.

So when he wanted to find out who Tess Showalter was and how she had found out about his plans, he knew just who to call. It took his source until Tuesday – Antonia Greco was famous for protecting her people, and this new investigative team of hers seemed particularly well shielded – but Dickens' source was persistent. And lucky. He had just happened to have dinner the previous night in Old Town Alexandria, in the same Italian restaurant where Tess Showalter and a nice-looking young man had gone out to celebrate her big story. A few clandestine photos of the pair canoodling, a tail back to their townhouse, and a little online research was all it took to nail it down.

As soon as Dickens ended the call, he sat back in his office chair and smiled evilly to himself. Antonia Greco was a worthy adversary indeed.

He picked up the phone again.

Harkness felt perverse relief when he saw Dickens' number come up on his phone. He, too, had seen the NWNN report on the march, and had been expecting – no, dreading – the call from the senator. Now that it was happening, he could stop worrying about it.

He was still scared to death. But at least he wasn't worried any more.

And yet, Dickens surprised him. Instead of raking him over the coals, Dickens demanded, "Harkness, did you know your girlfriend used to be bosom buddies with that Showalter girl's roommate?"

"Uh...well, no...that is..."

"And that the two of them are living in sin with that naval officer who was at the meeting on Friday?"

Harkness almost dropped the phone. "What?"

"There's a whole nest of 'em out there in the West End of Alexandria," Dickens growled. "And I'll bet you dollars to doughnuts that's how Antonia Greco found out about our meeting – from pillow talk between that little reporter girl and that officer."

"No bet, sir," Harkness said, groping for a chair. His guts were turning to water.

"Now, I'm going to do my level best to see that little viper's nest is broken up," Dickens went on. "But I want you to make sure your girlfriend is muzzled. Do you understand, Harkness? She is not to talk to anybody in the media from here on out. From now on, I want *you* to do all the talking. Is that understood?"

"B-but Senator," Harkness said, feeling the color drain from his face. "I thought we had agreed that I should stay out of the spotlight. Because of my record, you know."

"Hang your record," Dickens said. "Everybody already knows – it was all over NWNN. Didn't you see the report?"

"Yeah, I saw it," Harkness said miserably. "I just hate speaking to the press."

"Oh, for God's sake, Harkness. Just pretend they're your old parishioners, hungering for the Word of the Lord." The line went dead.

Harkness put away his phone, muttering, "Back then, I had a script."

Antonia ended her call thoughtfully. Then she sent Tess a message, asking her to come into her office.

"Hi, Antonia," Tess said from her doorway a minute later.

"Come on in and have a seat. Close the door."

Tess's eyebrows shot up, but she did as asked.

Antonia took a breath. "I just received a call from Senator Dickens. And it troubled me a little."

"Oh?"

She looked down at her desk for a moment. "Where did you get the information about the meeting last Friday night?" Before Tess could answer, she said, "And please be assured that the information will go no further than this office. I'm not going to divulge your source to Dickens or anybody else."

"Thank you," Tess said. "I heard about it from Darrell."

"And Darrell is...?" As Antonia said it, she realized that, other than what was on Tess's resume, and the impression she'd had upon their meeting that she was one of the gods' chosen, she didn't know much of anything about this woman.

"Lieutenant Darrell Warren. He's one of my housemates."

"You have another housemate, then?"

"Yeah. My college friend Sue. Why are you asking me this? What did Dickens say?"

Antonia sucked in another breath. "The senator said you were seen having dinner Monday night with Lieutenant Warren."

"Well, yeah. We went to Il Porto in Old Town after my story aired." Tess's forehead creased between her eyes. "Is that a problem?"

"Not unless there's more to your relationship," Antonia said.

Tess turned pink. "You mean, I shouldn't be sleeping with him."

"Not if he's a source, no."

The younger woman looked away. "If it makes any difference, we were nothing but housemates when he told me about the meeting."

Antonia risked a small smile. "That's a little better."

"But I should break it off."

Antonia's smile turned sad. "I'm afraid so."

Tess looked away again, but just for a moment. "What if I said that I don't intend to get any more information from him? And even if I did learn something from him, I wouldn't use it unless we can confirm it by another means?"

"Well...."

"That's not really any different from your relationship with Senator Holt, right?" Tess went on. "He might tell you something in confidence, but you don't go with it unless you get someone else to confirm it. Right?"

Antonia was about to say no, it wasn't like that at all. But she realized that it was exactly how she and Brock operated. In fact, TAaNA wouldn't have had the story about the march at all if it hadn't been for Brock eavesdropping on that conversation in the hallway a couple of weeks before.

She looked up at Tess – and there it was again. Just over Tess's shoulder was a shadowy female figure in leather armor and a black cloak. The shadow figure grinned at her; the Huntress in Antonia couldn't help but grin back. "All right, yes," she said. "I'll tell

Dickens there's nothing to his rumor, and he should keep his scummy accusations to himself from now on, or we'll dig up some dirt on *him.*"

Tess gave a wicked smile and rose to go. "Thanks, Antonia."

"Uh, Tess? One other thing." Tess cocked her head, waiting. "Your other housemate – Sue?"

"Sue Killeen," Tess supplied. "We went to Georgetown together."

"Right. Uh, she's not...involved with...?"

Tess made a face and laughed. "You mean, like, a threesome? Ugh, no!"

Antonia laughed, too. "Not that there's anything wrong with that."

"Yeah, no, of course not," Tess said. "Consenting adults, and all that. Just not with...ick. No." Then she blinked. "Is *that* what Dickens said to you?"

"He intimated it, yeah."

"Gack," said Tess, sticking her tongue out. "What a dirty-minded old bastard." She stood for a moment, considering. "If he brings it up again, Antonia? Tell him Sue and I have bedrooms upstairs, and Darrell has his own apartment in the basement. We share the kitchen and a half-bath, and that's it. If you want, you can come by and visit sometime to confirm it."

Antonia smiled. "That's okay, Tess. I appreciate the invitation, but I don't need to see for myself. I believe you."

Tess's smile was like sunshine. "Thanks, Antonia. You want your door open?"

"Sure."

Darrell finally got Tess to himself again late Wednesday night. She'd had to stay late at work to put together a couple of interviews they had done late in the day with one of her old Georgetown profs. The angle they were pursuing for Wednesday was an in-depth look at what made someone join a group like the True Believers. She told him she thought it was an interesting piece, although not as juicy as the original story on Monday.

That afternoon, they had run some comments from the executive director of NMAI. Tracie had finally convinced someone from the Smithsonian that the American Indian museum's festival was threatened. Tess said the Smithsonian spokeswoman also put them in touch with a Native American rights proponent; that was going to be their angle on Thursday. Friday afternoon, she would be live on the Mall to set the scene for the march and rally.

"Long week," he said.

"And it's going to get longer," she said. "I'll be down on the Mall all day Saturday. And then I have to write the wrap-up for Monday's show. But it feels so good to be _doing_ something finally, after all those weeks of spinning our wheels."

"Mmm," he said, brushing her shoulder with his fingertips. "I'll bet."

They were sharing his bed for the first time since Monday night. He was working his share of overtime this week, too. Today his unit had drilled with a fleet of kayaks at the marina in Lady Bird Park, across the Potomac from the Tidal Basin. He still had misgivings about the whole thing, and not just because of how ridiculous they would look – a bunch of camouflage-clad Navy men in bright orange plastic kayaks.

"I'll have to get video," Tess teased.

"You'll do no such thing," Darrell said, digging a finger into her side.

"Ow. But the pictures will be so great," she giggled. "Although I'll have to confirm it with somebody else before I can start the camera rolling. Hmm. Maybe we can just happen to stumble on the shot."

"What are you talking about?"

"Oh! I didn't get a chance to tell you." She rolled onto her stomach, presenting him with a distracting view of her naked ass. "Antonia called me into her office yesterday. That dirty old bastard, Senator Dickens, had called her because somebody told her they'd seen us at Il Porto Monday night."

Darrell couldn't help it. His hand found her ass of its own accord. "So what?" he asked. "Can't a guy take his girl out for dinner?"

"Am I your girl?" she asked, leaning in.

He kissed her. "Does that answer your question?" he asked, his lips against hers.

"Mmm. Maybe you'd better clarify that."

A little while later, he remembered that he'd never gotten an answer to his question. "So why _did_ Antonia want to know about us?"

"Well," she said, "it looks a little shady when a reporter's sleeping with a source."

He pushed himself up on one elbow to look at her. "Shady how?"

"Well," she said, "I guess it's like when a lobbyist pays for a congressman to go on an expensive trip or something, and then the congressman sponsors legislation that benefits the lobbyist's special interest group."

"It's an ethics violation," Darrell said slowly. "A *quid pro quo.*"

"Right. That's what it's called." She reached over and put her hand on his shoulder. "Hey, come over here."

"No, wait," he said. "I need to think about this."

"It's fine, Darrell," Tess said. "Antonia said it was fine. If you tell me anything, I have to check it out before we use it. We have to do the same thing if she finds out stuff from her husband."

He looked at her in the candlelight. She was beautiful. Enticing.

"And anyway," she went on, "we hadn't done anything before you told me about the meeting. It wasn't until afterward that we had sex the first time." She drew her fingers down his chest. "Stop worrying."

But something nagged at him. "So I'm a source, right? That's what you called me, isn't it?"

"Well, yeah, but...."

"Would you have slept with me if I didn't have any information you could use?"

She opened her mouth, but nothing came out.

"Who was your last boyfriend, Tess?" Darrell was starting to get angry. "How long ago?"

"Well...college, but..." she floundered. "But that was because of Sue being so crazy!"

"So I'm the first guy you could get something out of besides sex?"

"That's not how it was at all!" she said. "That's not why I slept with you!"

"Then why? To piss off Sue?" Darrell had begun trembling with anger. "Do you even care for me at all?"

"Do you even care for *me?*" she shot back. "Or am I just a convenient piece of ass to help you get over your ex-wife?" She threw herself off the bed and snatched up her clothes. "Don't answer that. I don't want to know." She disappeared through the curtain. Then his door slammed, and he heard her feet pounding up the stairs.

He got up and kicked the side of the mattress. Then he blew out the candles and lay back down in the dark. "Shit," he muttered. "Shit."

Tess flung herself onto her own narrow bed – the perfect size for a life of celibacy. Hot tears rolled down her cheeks and dripped onto her neck.

"Shall I wash his clothes for you?" Morrigan offered archly.

Tess gasped and sat up, clutching the sheet to her chest. "Get out!" she yelled.

"I shan't," the goddess said, and now Tess could see Her at the foot of the bed, lit dimly from the street light outside. "And I shan't wash his clothes, either, even if you wanted me to. We need him."

"*You* need him, is what You mean," Tess said bitterly.

"Perhaps," Morrigan said. "But we all have a long way to go before all of this is resolved. And he should not be encouraged to seek solace from his ex-wife. Not now."

Tess glared at Her. "Why?"

"It is not My place to say," Morrigan said.

"Well, I'm not gonna go back down there and make all nicey-nice with him so *he'll* tell me," she said. "Not unless You give me a good reason."

Morrigan gave her a measured look. Then She huffed a sigh. "I'll be back," She said, and faded away.

"Yeah, You do that," Tess said to the empty air.

It took her a few minutes to realize that this had been the first time she hadn't been cowed by Morrigan. "Maybe I should try getting pissed off more often," she said aloud.

And then she thought back to what Darrell had said. Did she care for him? Had she only slept with him because she knew Sue was interested?

"As if that mattered," Tess muttered. "It's not like he was interested in *her.*" Sighing, she turned over and made sure her alarm was set. Tomorrow was going to be another big day. She should probably be grateful that Darrell made her leave, so she could get a decent night's sleep instead of screwing like bunnies half the night.

Tears threatened again, but she swallowed them. "And Morrigan," she said aloud, "don't You come back tonight, either."

Either the goddess respected her wishes or never got the answer She went searching for; regardless, She did not, in fact, come back that night. Still, it was a long time before Tess drifted into a fitful sleep.

Chapter 15

Darrell walked up onto the back porch with a sense of relief. The last two days had been hell for him. When he was at work, he'd had trouble concentrating on his job – thoughts of Tess kept breaking his concentration, even when he needed to be most on the ball. Then at home the night before, when he was supposed to be getting ready for tonight's blessing ceremony, the logistics for Saturday morning's mission kept intruding on his preparations. And it didn't help that he was hypersensitive to any sounds coming from either of the two women who lived upstairs.

He was sure they were both treading lightly because of him, too. It was almost as if the house itself was holding its breath.

He sighed as he shut the door. He was home earlier than usual; Paulsen had dismissed them early to rest up. He needed to be at the marina at five hundred hours; the buses were supposed to start rolling up to the Washington Monument by seven hundred hours, and Paulsen wanted him to have his men in place near the Jefferson Memorial by then. He should, by rights, be heading to bed early, like the rest of his platoon. But no, he had promised to conduct a blessing ceremony that would take several hours.

Well, it was the least he could do for his relations. Especially since he was going to end up missing the troupe's performance.

The good news right now was that he was reasonably sure he would have the house to himself for the next several hours. Tess was at the Mall, he knew, getting ready to go on the air for her live report about the preparations for tomorrow; one of his co-workers had called him over when he saw her on a commercial earlier in the day. Darrell had grinned and tried to act as if nothing was wrong between the two of them. He wasn't sure whether he had pulled it off.

Sue, too, was likely at the Mall, taking care of last-minute details. She had been like a ghost all week, leaving for work earlier and coming home later than either Tess or him. The poor kittens never knew who was going to feed them at any given point.

Darrell was grateful that the cats' schedule hadn't suffered from his dust-up with Tess. Those little furry balls of trouble were perhaps the only living creatures in the place whose lives hadn't been disrupted by the discord.

Here they came now, insinuating themselves between his legs and demanding attention. He bent down to scratch behind their ears, saying, "If you guys think I'm going to feed you just because I'm home and I'm standing in the kitchen, you need to think again."

Mrs. Norris meowed indignantly and stalked off. Puck took a little longer to get discouraged; he stayed in the kitchen, watching, as Darrell headed through the living room and up the stairs. Since he had the place to himself, he decided to treat himself to a shower in his own home, for once.

He fetched a towel from the linen closet and paused. Both women had left their bedroom doors wide open. He peeked into Sue's, noting her altar and her neatly-made bed. Tess's room looked like a hurricane had hit it: clothing strewn haphazardly, items in a jumble on the dresser, and rumpled bedclothes with the pillows still bunched and twisted from what looked to him like a sleepless night.

Feeling suddenly like a voyeur, he locked the bathroom door and showered rapidly, trying not to think about either of the women who had stood naked under the same spray of water just a few hours earlier.

Back downstairs in his apartment, he breathed deeply for a few beats, letting go of his trouble with Tess and his misgivings about the next day's mission. Then he carefully dressed in his ceremonial outfit: the leggings, robe, and headdress of the *midew*, his erstwhile profession.

"It suits you," Nanabush said from His perch on the bed.

Darrell turned to regard Him briefly. "It has always suited me. Too bad Somebody thought it would be a better idea for me to join the Navy."

"Hey, you got to see the world," the god offered.

Darrell cocked his head and gave Him a look that meant, *Nice try.* Then he began packing up his kit.

Undaunted, Nanabush said, "So I guess Ruthie will be there tonight, huh?"

"I guess," he said shortly. Ruthie was another topic he didn't want to dwell on just now.

But the god had an agenda. "Look, Darrell," He said. "We're worried about her."

"Oh? Why?"

"We talked it over." The god sounded distinctly uncomfortable. "We think Lucifer might intend to use her tomorrow."

Darrell frowned and turned to him. "Use her how?"

Nanabush spread His upturned hands. "I wish I knew. Just keep an eye on her, okay? And watch yourself around her."

"Why?" Darrell asked, amused. "You think she might try to turn me to the dark side?"

"You never know. I hear they have cookies," Nanabush grinned. Then He sobered. "Just be careful."

"Stop it," Darrell said. "You're creeping me out, and I need to concentrate for this." He started to duck through the curtain. Then he stopped and turned back. "Will You be there tonight?"

"I am everywhere, all the time," Nanabush said, making His voice go deep. "Cookie?"

Darrell snorted and let the curtain fall.

Puck was still waiting in the kitchen when Darrell emerged from the basement. The cat took one look at this stranger who was robed and feathered to within an inch of his life, and fled.

Tess hated these kinds of assignments. Here she was, in front of a building where nothing was happening, trying to sound enthusiastic while she described what would be happening *right here where I'm standing! But not until tomorrow!*

At least Sue had agreed to do a quick Q-&-A with her. Tess thought Earth Power Week had gotten short shrift in all the cowboys-and-Indians hoopla. She wanted her viewers to understand that people besides just the marchers and the festival-goers would be down here, too. And she thought maybe if Heather saw Tess's report, she would realize that innocent people could be hurt in this manufactured crisis and call it off. She wasn't hopeful, but she figured it was worth a shot.

Sue showed up at the appointed time, looking tired and sweaty. Tess was sweaty, too, for that matter – the weather in D.C. had turned hot and humid just in time for all the craziness. She wasn't surprised; it was August, after all, and legend had it that Washington was built on a swamp. But still, it would have been nice not to have to worry about damp spots on her clothing showing up on camera. She hoped Sue would perk up when the camera was on her.

Tess listened to Antonia's lead-in in her earpiece, and picked up her cue smoothly. She blathered on about the upcoming events that would be happening *right here where I'm standing* for about twenty seconds, and then she turned to her housemate. "But the True Believers' march and the NMAI festival aren't the only things happening on the Mall this weekend. The nonprofit group Earth in Balance will also be wrapping up its annual Earth Power Week. Here with me is the assistant director of Earth in Balance and project manager for Earth Power Week, Sue Killeen. Sue, thanks for joining us."

"Sure thing, Tess." Sue sounded relaxed, but she looked stiff. Tess realized belatedly that she was probably worried about losing her sunhat, which she'd been wearing all day. Schuyler had asked her at first to take it off because her eyes disappeared under it, but then he realized she had a serious case of hat hair and told her to put it back on. As a compromise, Sue had scooted the hat back so that it sat at a rakish angle. That kept her eyes unshaded, mostly, but now she was in danger of having the thing fly off on national television.

Tess rolled her eyes mentally and plowed onward. "Give us a little rundown of the exhibits you've had here this week. These windmills behind us – are they part of the show?"

Obligingly, Sue explained how the devices were actually scaled down versions of the ones used in industrial power-generating applications, but that they really did work. "We were pretty sure that between the wind turbines and the solar panels, we would generate enough power for our own use. But our demonstration project has been such a success that we've actually been able to sell power to Pepco."

"That's wonderful," Tess said. "Now what about this little house over here? Tell us about that."

As Sue explained about the solar-powered house, Schuyler gave Tess the sign for thirty seconds left. Tess broke in when Sue took her next breath, hoping she didn't seem too rude to the folks at home, and asked another question. "How many visitors have you had this week?"

"It's hard to tell. The show is free to enter, so we don't have a way of generating exact attendance numbers," Sue said. "But I'd estimate we've probably had several thousand people walk through over the course of the week."

"Several thousand," Tess said. "And I would imagine the crowd will be bigger tomorrow."

"Oh, sure. Saturday is always our busiest day of the show."

"Are you worried about the impact of the march on the busiest day of your show?"

Sue expression turned serious. "Well, of course we are," she said. "Solar panels aren't cheap, and neither are these wind turbines. Any time you get a big crowd, you're concerned about carelessness, or worse. And too, the marchers could perceive *us* as a threat."

"How so?" Tess asked as Schuyler began the final countdown.

"Well, it's obvious, isn't it?" Sue said. "We're crunchy-granola hippies to them. As far as they're concerned, we're part of the problem, just as much as the Native Americans are."

Tess waited a beat for that to sink in to the minds of Mr. and Mrs. America. Then she said, "Well, I hope you and your show survive the weekend without any damage. Sue Killeen with Earth in Balance, thanks for being here with us." She turned to the camera and said, "So Antonia, it could be a very interesting weekend down here on the National Mall – for a lot of people."

"Indeed, it could. Thank you, Tess," she heard Antonia say in her earpiece. "All of us here at NWNN hope everyone survives the weekend without any mishaps. Coming up next on TAaNA...."

"And we're out," Schuyler said. "Thanks, ladies."

Tess yanked out her earpiece and handed it to him. Then she turned to Sue. "Seriously, how's it going?"

"Okay," Sue said. "We really have had a lot of traffic this week. I don't know whether it's the wind turbines pulling them in, or the run-up to the march tomorrow."

"Any publicity is good publicity," Tess said with a grin. "You're welcome."

"Did you hear that the mayor tried to talk the Park Service into rescinding the permit?"

Tess snorted. "Yeah. Unfortunately, the First Amendment is still in full force and effect, which means Americans still have the right to say any damn stupid thing they please in a public place."

"At least he convinced the march organizers to make sure their people weren't packing heat," Schuyler said. "Although I wouldn't place any bets on how carefully they'll check for guns."

"I wouldn't, either," said Tess.

"Gods, it's hot out here," Sue said, pulling on the neckline of her shirt. "Want to come into my trailer and cool off? I've got a fridge stocked with water and sodas for the interns."

"Ooh, that sounds divine. But we've got one more live shot before we wrap up, and I need to go round up the guy from the Smithsonian who's supposed to talk to us."

"Well, stop by when you're done, if you have time," Sue said. "At least come by and grab a cold drink. Just go in and help yourselves if I'm not there. I don't want you guys passing out from dehydration."

"Me, neither," Schuyler said. "Thanks for the offer, Sue. Nice to meet you."

"Nice to meet you, too," she smiled. "Take care. Tess, I'll see you at home tonight."

"Tonight?" Tess said with a laugh. "More like Sunday."

Sue laughed as well. "Good point. I fully intend to sleep for forty-eight hours straight when this is all over."

As Sue walked toward her makeshift office, she hailed one of the engineers working at the event. "Do me a favor and make sure your crew double-checks all the tie-downs on the exhibits before you leave tonight," she told him.

"Of course," the man said. "We have a checklist that we've been following every night this week."

"Well, double-check the checklist, then," she said. "We're liable to be overrun by nutjobs tomorrow, and I don't want any of these wind turbines to fall on them." She grinned. "Unless they do something to deserve it."

The man smiled. "Got it, boss."

As soon as she got back to the trailer, she called Denise. "How's the planning coming, lieutenant?" she joked.

Denise laughed. "All present and accounted for, sir. I talked to Becca a little while ago. It looks like we may have more than five hundred people."

"Wow, that's great news," Sue said. "Sounds like we'll be able to surround the whole Mall."

"I was thinking about that," her friend said. "We should have enough to reach from the west side of the Washington Monument to the west side of the Capitol, and from Constitution to Independence."

"Sweet. I approve," Sue said. "Both the museum and my show would be covered."

"I'm going to put myself at the Capitol Reflecting Pool," Denise went on. "I want Becca as far from the action as possible, so I think she and Tim should stay near the national phallic symbol. Where do you want to be?"

"I'll be at the American Indian museum," she said. "I want to be near the show, just in case anything blows up."

"Okay," Denise said. "You're on Independence. Then Sammy can be our anchor on 17th, and Joanie can be on Constitution." She paused. "You know what? I think this is going to work."

Sue grinned. "Oh, I know it will work. The gods are on our side."

An hour later, Tess and Schuyler dragged themselves up the metal stairs to Sue's office trailer and knocked on the door. When no one answered, they looked at each other. "Maybe we should just go," Schuyler said.

"No way," said Tess, who had run out of water a half-hour before. "I'm dying here. She said we could go in and help ourselves." She turned the knob and opened the door – and surprised a young man in the act of rifling through Sue's desk.

"Um," Tess said. "Are you supposed to be doing that?"

"Yeah! Yeah, I'm an intern. Sue needed a pen and...."

Schuyler pointed to the cupful of pens on the corner of the desk. "Would one of those do?"

"Yeah! Hey, thanks!" The guy grabbed a pen from the cup and slung an orange backpack over his shoulder. Then he did a little dance to get past Tess and Schuyler in the cramped space.

"What's your name?" Tess called as he opened the door.

"Jim. Jim Steinbaugh. Nice to meet you!" The kid nodded brightly and slammed the door behind him. The floor vibrated as he tore down the stairs.

"That was weird," Schuyler observed.

"Yeah, it was." Tess stared at the door. "I wonder if he had any business being in here. I'll have to ask Sue."

"Call her," Schuyler suggested.

"Won't do any good," Tess said, pointing into the drawer the kid had left open when he ran out. "Her phone's right there. I'll talk to her tonight at home. What?" she said to Schuyler's puzzled look.

"He didn't take her phone?"

She shrugged. "I guess not."

"What was he after, then?"

"That," Tess said, "is an excellent question."

Chapter 16

The refreshments, courtesy of EiB, barely made a dent. Tess and Schuyler were still hot and tired when they returned to the studio from their long afternoon on the Mall. "Man, that heat is brutal," Schuyler said as they unloaded the car. "All I want is a shower and bed."

Super-cooled air blasted them as they entered the building, and Tess stopped for a moment, eyes shut in relief. "Ahhh. Me, too. I hope they don't expect us to do anything else tonight."

But Tracie had left her a note about a planning meeting for the next day's coverage. Tess glanced at the time, sighed heavily, and joined her friend in the conference room where Antonia was detailing the assignments.

"We'll set up a command post on the Capitol grounds," Antonia was saying. "Max and I will anchor the coverage from there." She nodded at Max Parrish, one of the regular afternoon news anchors. "I want three reporting teams on the Mall." She wrote the names on her tablet, and they showed up on the screen behind her. "Ned Ainsworth will cover from the Capitol." That made sense to Tess; the Capitol was Ned's beat. "Heela Shahin will be stationed on the Mall at the museum. And Tess Showalter will start at the Washington Monument and walk along with the marchers."

"Wait a minute," Tess said. "The action's going to be at the museum."

"Right," Antonia said. "And you'll get there when the march does."

"But it's my story," she persisted, cutting a look at Heela. "It's been my story all along, not hers. No offense, Heela, but I want to be at the Mall."

Heela waved. "None taken. Put me wherever, Antonia."

"Tess, you'll get more airtime if you're with the marchers," Max put in.

Tess stared at him for a moment. "I don't care about airtime," she said. "I care about covering the story. The march is going to be B-roll, Max. The story will be at the museum."

Antonia regarded them all for a moment. "All done?" she inquired mildly. "Let me sleep on it. I'll let the two of you know in the morning."

Heela nodded. "Fine with me."

"Tess?" Antonia looked at her, eyebrows raised.

She opened her mouth to keep arguing, but Tracie put a hand on her forearm and shook her head slightly. "Fine," she grumbled.

"Thank you," Antonia said, as much to Tracie as to Tess. "Be at the command center at 6:30 in the morning. And don't forget to wear your sunscreen. The forecast for tomorrow is hazy, hot and humid."

"Terrific," Tess muttered to Tracie. "Another sweaty day. And I might have to walk for blocks alongside crazy people."

Tracie patted her on the shoulder. "It won't be as bad tomorrow," she said. "We're starting early. We could be nearly done by the time the heat really ramps up. Maybe Antonia will let you go home early."

"Fat chance," Tess told her. "We're in this 'til the bitter end. Better bring lots of water."

Darrell arrived early at the hotel where the tribe was staying. He checked the time on the clock in his dashboard and grunted, pleased. He would need some time to set up, anyway.

He received some odd looks from hotel guests as he crossed the parking lot. *I guess it's not every day that they see an honest-to-God Indian around these parts.* And then he realized they might be wondering where the costume party was.

Inside, he approached the desk clerk on duty, and was grateful when the man pointed him to the meeting room the tribe had reserved without commenting on his getup. He remembered to ask whether lighting candles in the room would cause a problem with the smoke detector.

"It shouldn't. But if you're really worried, you could open a window," the man said.

"Thanks," said Darrell. "I'll do that, just to make sure. I wouldn't want to cause the whole hotel to be evacuated."

"And we appreciate that," the man said.

The meeting room was on the second floor. He attracted more stares from the people who rode up in the elevator with him. He smiled at them briefly, and then looked straight ahead until the doors opened. *Being a medicine man sure is a whole 'nother experience off the rez.*

The room was adequate for his plans. He opened the windows a crack. Then he scooted all the tables back and folded up the chairs, to give him a large area to work in. Toward the southern part of the room, he set up a group of candles; being indoors and lacking a fire pit, the candles would stand in for their ceremonial fire. Then he removed a braid of sweetgrass from his kit and lit it. Singing softly to the manitous – the Anishinaabe gods and spirits – he worked his way around the room, smudging the ceremonial space to purify it.

By the time he had accomplished all of that, his cousin Mike had arrived. As teenagers, Darrell and Mike had looked very much alike. But Darrell noted that while his Navy duties had required him to keep in top physical form, Mike was developing a bit of a spare tire.

Still, it was good to see him. Mike put down the drum he had brought and the men embraced. "It's good to see you, cuz," Mike said as he stepped back. "You look great."

"So do you," said Darrell. "I've missed you, cuz."

"We've missed you, too. Gus says hi."

Darrell grinned at the thought of his old mentor. "I bet he deliberately stayed home so I'd have to put on this getup again. You should have seen the looks I got in the parking lot."

Mike laughed. "Wait 'til we leave for the museum tomorrow. Bad enough to have one wild Indian stalking the place. Tomorrow, there'll be five or six of us."

Darrell's smile turned wistful. "I wish I could see it. I have some bad news, cuz. I've got to work tomorrow. I can't come to see the dance."

Mike was clearly crestfallen, although he tried not to show it. "Well. You've gotta do what you've gotta do, I guess. Maybe we can give you a little private performance tonight."

"That would be great."

At that point, the other members of the troupe began arriving. Darrell held up a hand to stop them from entering and turned to Mike. "Want to do the honors on the drum?"

"I thought you'd never ask," his cousin said with a big grin. He snatched up the drum while Darrell relit the sweetgrass. Then Darrell smudged the two of them, and as Mike began to drum and sing, Darrell wafted the smoke over each of the dancers as they entered the room.

The last to enter was Ruthie.

He noticed everything about her: the contours of her face, her hesitant posture, the way she looked at him with her liquid brown eyes. She might have been trembling as he smudged her; goodness knew it was all he could do to hold his own hands steady.

"Darrell," she whispered as he finished, and gave him a tentative smile.

He stood there, smiling at her like a fool. He wanted to touch her. He couldn't touch her, or he'd never finish the ceremony.

"I quit gambling," she said shyly. He felt his smile grow wider. "And it's different this time," she went on, encouraged by his expression. "You were right. I'm more peaceful without it." She put a hand on his forearm before going to stand next to the others in the troupe.

He stood frozen for a moment. *I made a difference. She listened to me. Oh, Ruthie....*

Then he recollected himself and walked to his kit, where his pipe lay. This wasn't the tribe's peace pipe – that sacred item had never been in his possession. Gus had given him this one just before he left for the Navy. He had almost turned it down, but his mentor had insisted: *Maybe you'll need it for a ceremony someday.* Darrell blessed the man's foresight.

He lit the pipe himself because the group had not brought an official Fire Keeper. He then held it aloft and asked for the blessing of Gitchi Manitou, the Great Mystery, and of Mizzu Kummick Quae, Mother Earth. He turned then to the North, West, South, and East, asking the spirits of the directions to bless the gathering. And finally, he appealed to Makataeshigun, the Spirit of the Underworld, to look kindly upon them, and to stay far away from them while they sought peace.

Darrell spoke all these requests in Potawatomi. He was pleasantly surprised at how easily the words of the chants came back to him. Maybe it was the clothing he was wearing that jogged his memory, or maybe it was being in this room with these people who depended on him to do it right.

And as he spoke, a strange thing happened. The walls surrounding them fell away; the carpet became springy grass; oaks and maples arched over their heads; and a real fire replaced his candles. The sacred space he had created became real.

As the dancers looked around in surprise, he asked them to put any offerings they might have brought next to the ceremonial fire. A few people did. Some had brought small packets of tobacco; others brought a message on paper that was then rolled up like a scroll. Ruthie was among those who left a scroll next to the fire.

Then Mike began drumming again, and Darrell called out to the manitous to bless the dancers during their performance. "Let them represent our band and our heritage well," he said. "Let them teach the people who are not of our band about our culture, so that they will come to appreciate it and not fear us. Let them perform in safety and let them return home safely."

Nanabush, hovering in the back of the room, smiled and nodded.

Mike then began singing one of the songs the dancers would be performing the next day, and the group exploded into movement. Even without their costumes, Darrell thought, it was a wonderful sight.

Ruthie laughed and caught his hand, pulling him into the dance. Around the fire they moved, weaving in and out between one another, spiraling in and then out again. Shadowy presences danced along with them; Darrell saw Pukawiss, Nanabush's brother who invented dancing, in His elegant costume, and other manitous as well. He laughed and sang with his friends, and his hand never left Ruthie's. He hadn't felt so carefree since he'd left home for Officer Candidate School.

Finally, Mike's drumming ceased, the wooded glade fading away with the drum's final vibration. But the smiles of wonder on the faces of his relations were real. Wearing his own big smile, Darrell broke away from the dancers and said, "And now, we feast!"

It wasn't much of a feast — the dancers had been on the road all day so there had been little time to prepare anything. But there was a wild rice dish someone had brought from home, and sandwich fixings from a grocery store near the hotel, and several types of berries for dessert. And there was laughter.

Ruthie never left his side. She stayed until even Mike had left, blowing out the candles and closing the windows while Darrell packed up his kit. And then she put her arms around him, under his ceremonial tunic, and kissed him.

Staying with her that night seemed, to him, like the most logical thing in the world.

And yet he had to leave so early. He had told her so the night before, as they were shedding their clothes. But either she hadn't heard him or she hadn't wanted to understand.

Now she sat up in the hotel bed, wearing the same look he had seen on her face countless times before. As he watched her, his heart sinking, he realized he was comparing her to Tess. Ruthie wasn't as petite as Tess, and her face was more striking than cute. But he *knew* Ruthie, down to the smallest fiber of her being. At one time in his life, she had suited him completely. Then he had convinced himself that they had never been suited. Now he found himself wondering if he hadn't been right to start with. And he cursed the Navy and all the senators on Capitol Hill for keeping him from further exploration of the question right now.

"I'm really sorry," he said to her as he put on his ceremonial outfit again – the only clothes he had with him. "I want to stay. But I have to go."

He was braced for a tantrum, but to his surprise, none came. "Duty calls," she said dully. "Will I see you again after you get off work? Or tomorrow?"

"Tomorrow, for sure," he said, and leaned across the bed to kiss her again. She put her arms around his neck and pulled him close. Against his will, he gently loosened her arms and repeated, "Tomorrow, for sure."

The household was quiet as he let himself in the back door; apparently even the cats were still asleep. He made his way downstairs and carefully put away his regalia. His heart hurt as he closed the lid on the trunk. After last night and its magic, he was sure he knew where he belonged – and it wasn't rowing across the Potomac at sunrise, carrying a gun.

And yet he knew where he had to be.

"Duty calls," he said, in the same tone of resignation Ruthie had used. He dressed in his fatigues and went back out to his car.

As he drove to the marina, torturing himself with memories of the night just past, he recalled what Nanabush had said to him – about how Lucifer might be planning to use Ruthie against him. He shook his head. Sure, the two of them had had their ups and downs over the years, but he could swear she had never had an evil bone in her body. Even last night, he hadn't had a sense that she was anything other than what he had always believed her to be: a good woman who had the misfortune of being mixed up with him.

"You're wrong about her," he said aloud.

Nanabush didn't deign to reply. Sighing, he kept going through the darkness.

Sue hit the snooze button. Then she heard the back door open, and sat up. She weighed whether to go downstairs and talk to Darrell, but by the time she had showered and dressed, he was gone again.

It was just as well, she thought, as she started the coffee and filled the cats' kibble bowl. She didn't really know what to say to him. Her initial anger was dissipating, and she was beginning to wonder whether he had a point. Maybe she *was* too quick to cry victimhood. Maybe she ought to think about looking for dates as far away from Tess as possible.

And then she thought of Sammy and the way he looked at her with puppy-dog devotion, and made a face.

She heard a soft rap on the front door, and went to open it. "You're early," she told Denise, stepping aside to let her in.

"Couldn't sleep. And anyway, I had to pick up the copies of the chant." She held a cup of coffee in one hand; with her other arm, she clutched a box from the twenty-four-hour copy place. "I had them print a thousand, just in case. I brought this box in so we could look at them. The other box is still in the car."

"You really think we'll get that many people?" Sue asked, taking the box to the table and opening it. "These look great. Breakfast?" She sat down to finish her cereal.

"I'm good, thanks."

"I thought I heard voices," said Tess from the stairs. "Hey, Denise."

"Hey, sleepyhead," Denise grinned. "Are you going to be in on all the fun today, too? I caught part of your show yesterday. You looked good."

"Thanks," Tess said with a yawn. "Yeah, I'll be right there in the thick of it, one way or the other."

"What does that mean?" asked Sue.

"Oh, Antonia was being a bitch yesterday," Tess said, waving in dismissal. "I may have to arm-wrestle Heela to get a spot near the museum. But it'll all work out."

"I guess I'll see you at the museum, then," Sue said, putting her bowl in the kitchen sink. "That's where I'll be, too. Coffee's ready if you want some."

"Thanks, but I think I'll take a shower first. Um. Have you seen Darrell this morning?"

Sue frowned. "No. He came in and left again before I got down here."

"He was out all night?" Tess asked.

"I guess so. I figured you knew about it," Sue said carefully.

Tess shook her head. Sue wondered at the look on her face. "Well," Tess said, "I'll see you both down there, I guess." And she went back upstairs.

"What's that all about?" Denise asked.

Sue sighed. "What do you think it's about? She's sleeping with the guy."

"Y'all's housemate? Convenient." Denise glanced back toward the stairs.

Sue could hear the shower running. "Yeah, for somebody. Come on – let's go."

The sky was beginning to lighten to the east as they climbed into Denise's car. "Look," Denise said as she pulled away from the curb, "it's none of my business, but y'all have been dysfunctional friends for as long as I've known you. Why don't you move out?"

Sue turned to her in surprise. "What? Why?"

"Because I think you'd be happier if you weren't living where Tess could parade her sex life under your nose every chance she gets. And so would she."

"You think she does it to me deliberately?"

Denise glanced at her. "You must have missed the part where I said *both* of you are dysfunctional."

"You think I play the victim," Sue said quietly.

"That's not what I said."

"No, that's what Darrell said."

Denise glanced at her again. "The new housemate? He said that to you? What an asshole. Can you kick him out?"

Sue laughed. "Not really. We need his rent money."

"Girl, you can find another housemate. I'm serious. I'd kick his ass out."

"I'll think about it," Sue said, so Denise would drop it. She had no intention of kicking Darrell out. The gods wanted them all together for a reason. She just hoped Their reason, when she learned it, would justify all of this.

Tess stood under the tap, unmoving, until the water started to get cold.

So Darrell was out all night. With his friends from home. She supposed she could grant him that. *Maybe they just got to talking and reminiscing, and he lost track of the time. And he just stayed there, rather than driving home, since he had to be up so early anyway.*

A treacherous part of her mind – the part that always second-guessed her on everything – suggested that maybe he hadn't stayed out all night with *all* of his friends. Maybe he'd been with just one of them. *What was her name? Ruthie, wasn't it?*

She shut off the water and stepped out of the shower. He hadn't said a word to her about his ex-wife coming to town.

Well, he wouldn't, would he?

She banged a fist on the door. Then she straightened. "Stop sniveling," she told what she could see of herself in the foggy mirror. "It's not like we had an exclusive relationship. It's not like we really had a relationship at all. We only went out on one actual date. He can see whoever he wants."

It doesn't mean it doesn't hurt, though.

As she dressed, she wondered how people ever got to the point where they could settle down with someone. It just seemed like relationships were fraught with too much angst to ever work out.

Chapter 17

Shortly before 6:00 a.m., a fleet of kayaks – dark green, not day-glo orange – glided silently across the Potomac to the Tidal Basin inlet. A few minutes later, the paddlers beached their craft on the inlet's left bank and made their way to the Jefferson Memorial.

Darrell and his men waited in the shadows. Sunrise was just a few minutes away, but although the sky was brightening, it was too dark inside the memorial to read any of the words chiseled on the interior walls. Darrell checked the time on his phone and saw that the buses wouldn't begin arriving for at least another forty-five minutes. He dropped to a crouch and settled in to wait.

Not long after, Denise pulled her car into a parking spot on a side street just off Constitution Avenue Northwest. Carrying the boxes from the printer, the women crossed Constitution and headed for its intersection with 17th Street.

A few people were already there: Becca and Tim, sharing a thermos of tea, and several people Sue didn't recognize. Becca introduced them, and Sue shook hands and thanked them for coming, but their names didn't stick in her head. Denise started handing out copies of the chant.

More people arrived, including Sammy. "What can I do?" he asked immediately. "I haven't seen any buses yet."

Sue squinted against the glare as the sun cleared the tops of the buildings to their east. "They won't be here until seven or so. Just hang out, I guess. Or here – pass out some flyers." She grabbed a stack from Denise and handed them over.

He grinned and saluted. "Aye aye, captain, ma'am." Then he wandered off.

Denise was smiling. "He's quite a character, our Sammy."

"That's one way to put it," Sue said. But she smiled, too.

The crowd kept growing. Joanie glanced around as she reported in. "Wow. I didn't know we had this many Pagans in D.C."

Just then, Sammy returned. "Hey, Joanie," he said. "Denise, I need more flyers."

"We're out," Denise said. "I just gave the last of them to a Pagan group from Baltimore."

"We've got a group from Baltimore?" Sue asked, stunned.

"That's what the lady said. And I met another group that came from Philly." Denise clapped her hands to get everyone's attention. "Hey, y'all, listen up," she yelled. "Can we get a little quiet, here? Our captain has a few words for us." As the crowd fell silent, Denise turned to Sue. "You're on, captain, ma'am."

"I'll get you for this," Sue said quietly, which sent Denise off into gales of laughter. She climbed partway up the rise to the monument and turned to face the crowd. "Good morning, everyone!" Sue called out, grateful for her height, for once. "Thank you all for coming today. We certainly didn't expect such a big turnout, but we're glad you came, and we can sure use your help.

"As you may have heard, there's going to be a big march and rally on the Mall today. It's sponsored by a group of deniers and an anti-Native American group. They'll be gathering on the south side of the Washington Monument and marching down Independence to the Capitol. Now, there's also a festival going on at the American Indian museum today, and we've heard there may be some violence. And there's an alternative power festival on the Mall. Can you see the wind turbines above the trees? That's it.

"So what we're going to do is cast a protective circle around the Mall, from here down to Independence, then east to the American Indian museum and the Capitol, and back up Constitution to here. It'll be more like a rectangle, I guess, but we're hoping the gods won't stiff us on a technicality." She smiled, and saw some smiles in response. *Good – I haven't lost them.* "What I'd like to do now is to run through the chant a few times, to make sure we've got it down pat. If you don't have a copy, share with a friend. It's only two lines, so you should be able to memorize it pretty fast. Since this is the District of Columbia, we'll be petitioning Columbia. That's Her statue on top of the Capitol dome. We think She's as close to a goddess of this place as we're likely to find.

"We're going to keep repeating the chant while we walk deosil along the perimeter. Tim here will be leading us. Wave to the nice Pagans, Tim." Tim obliged, to giggles; a few people waved back. "Becca will be our anchor. When she sees Tim in position, she'll stop chanting and call out down the street that the circle is cast. When you hear that, pass it on to the next person. And then stay in position.

"Then at nine o'clock on the dot, when the marchers step off, I want to renew the chant, just to make sure our circle is really tight. So please set an alarm on your watch or your phone for 9:00 a.m. right now. When the alarm rings, start chanting again, and repeat the chant three times. When it's all over, Denise will send a message down the line that the circle is broken. Then you're free to go home. That should do it. Okay? Okay. Let's try the chant." She borrowed a copy from someone in the front row and read aloud:

Lady Columbia, we ask You for Your aid.
Protect this place and keep all its people safe.

Becca had written it. The lines didn't quite rhyme, but Sue hoped that, like their rectangular "circle," it would get the job done.

She had the crowd read through the chant three times, exhorting them to get louder each time, until everyone was practically shouting. "Okay!" she said at last.

Then Denise took over. Holding aloft a bottle of water and a slice of bread, she cried, "Behold us, Lady Goddess, and all the gods and goddesses! We give you this offering. Bless us and our purpose here today. Our goal is clear and just. May our strength never waver." She broke the bread into small pieces and scattered them under a tree; then she poured most of the water onto the ground beside the bread. "So mote it be," she said.

"So mote it be," Sue repeated. Then she took a breath. "Tim?"

He squeezed Becca's hand and began walking down 17th Street, chanting at the top of his lungs. Sue took a spot in the middle of the group, shouting for all she was worth; Denise stationed herself at the rear and put herself in charge of positioning people along the route.

As the group passed the American Indian museum, Sue peeled off and took up her position across the street from the entrance. She kept chanting as the group went past, pumping her fist and clapping, and encouraged those near her to keep going. Not long after, word reached her that the circle was complete. She passed the message down the line. Then she reached for a water bottle. The sun was nowhere near its zenith, but she was already sweating.

As the Pagans were beginning to cast their circle, Tess arrived at the NWNN command center. A crew had already assembled the mobile studio Antonia and Max would use. Antonia herself was inside the command center, holding a briefing book and chatting with her husband, Senator Holt, who stood next to her chair.

"Tess! There you are," she said.

"Hi, Antonia. Senator." She nodded to him. "Where do you want me to be today?"

Antonia stood and approached her. "Listen," she said in a low voice, "I'm sorry if I upset you yesterday. I didn't mean to, but I was just trying to keep you safe. I'm really worried that this thing today could turn violent, and Heela has experience in a war zone."

"I'll be fine," Tess insisted.

Antonia sighed, regarding her with affection. "I know you will. Diana made Morrigan promise to take care of you." As Tess's jaw dropped, she went on, "Go on, get out of here. Tracie and Schuyler are already setting up by the museum."

"I've got to go," Senator Holt said, leaning in to kiss his wife. "See you later, honey. Knock 'em dead." Then he wrapped an arm around Tess's shoulders and said in her ear, "You, too."

Tess was still too blindsided by Antonia's words to protest. After the senator left, she turned back to her boss and said, "So wait. Diana spoke to Morrigan."

"Uh-huh."

"And Morrigan didn't give Her a hard time."

Antonia snorted. "I never said *that.*"

Heaving a gusty sigh of relief, Tess said, "Thanks, Antonia. I promise not to screw up." Her heart singing, she nearly ran the two blocks to the museum.

She found her team leaning against a tree near the entrance. "Gonna be another scorcher," Schuyler said. "I brought extra water from the command center for us."

"You're amazing," Tess said, and dove for a bottle, downing half of it at once. She looked across the street and spied Sue, her big sunhat flopping in the slight breeze. "So what do we do now?"

Tracie shrugged. "Wait, I guess."

Across the street, Sue was beginning to wonder whether they had gotten into position too early. The temperature was climbing with the sun. At least a third of the water in her bottle was gone, and the march hadn't even started yet.

She looked west, down the street where the marchers would be coming from, and spotted a familiar figure coming toward her. "Oh, gods," she muttered. "What's he doing here?"

Jim Steinbaugh, the intern she had sent away the other day, was back. "Hi, Sue!" he said, smiling broadly. "I'm here to help out. What can I do?"

"You can go back home," she said.

"But Freda said..." he began.

Sue made a mental note to speak to her boss on Monday about overriding her decisions. "Freda's not in charge of this project. I am. And I don't want you within five miles of here today. Go home."

"But who's looking after the show if you're stuck out here?" he asked. "I could head over there right now. I know what to do."

"Look, I'm going to level with you," she said. "In case you hadn't heard, a whole group of anti-Native American marchers is going to come through here in a little while, and this place is liable to go up like a powder keg. Now, you said some pretty nasty things about Indians the other day, and...."

"You must have misunderstood me. All I meant was...."

Sue held up a hand. "I don't care. I know what I heard. And I heard enough to know that I don't want you on my project." She tapped him on the chest with a forefinger. "Got that? There is no place for bigotry in my world, and that includes at work. That's why I sent you back to the office, and that's why I'm telling you to leave right now. There are already going to be too many loose cannons down here today."

The young man gave her a hard look. Then he walked away, throwing over his shoulder, "You'll be sorry for this, Sue."

"I doubt it," she muttered, watching him to make sure he actually left. When he turned the corner toward L'Enfant Plaza, his orange backpack bobbing as he walked, she breathed a sigh of relief.

A few minutes later, a van pulled up near the museum's side entrance, and Sue saw a number of people pile out. Some wore embroidered costumes and moccasins. "That must be Darrell's friends," she said aloud, and thought of going over to introduce herself. But then she remembered she needed to stay to hold the circle at least until the march began. And anyway, they went inside too quickly; she would never have made it over there in time.

"Hey," Schuyler said, pointing across the street. "Isn't that the guy we saw rifling Sue's desk?"

Tess looked where he was pointing. "Shit. It is. And I forgot to tell her about him." She moved to cross the street, but Tracie frantically waved her back.

"Where are you going?" she hissed. "You need to stay here in case something happens!"

Milton Harkness and Heather Willis stood in the sunshine on the sidewalk at 15th and Independence, waiting for the buses. A few steps away, several D.C. police officers stood around a table, ready to check the bus passengers' bags.

The air felt unwelcoming somehow. Harkness figured it was the heat. "Eighty degrees at seven o'clock in the morning," he kept saying. "It gets hot at home, but not like this."

"Shut up, Milton," Heather finally snapped at him, revealing that she was feeling the stress, too. She was wearing a stylish sunhat, which looked a little odd with her form-fitting t-shirt and capris. The outfit revealed a little too much of her luscious shape, he thought, but he wasn't about to reopen that discussion. At first, Heather had intended to wear a halter top and skort, but Harkness told her that too many of his followers would think she was a harlot.

"Aren't I?" she had said, and...but that memory was for another time. Not now, while he was trying to look professional and leader-like, even though he was wilting inside his seersucker suit.

"Here they come," Heather said with relief. For the next hour or so, they split up, monitoring the bag check, showing the marchers where to wait, and going over the plans again with the leaders of the out-of-town groups.

As the clock ticked toward nine and the row of buses dwindled, Heather tallied the numbers on her manifest and frowned. "I thought you rented a hundred seventy-five buses," she said.

"I did," he responded. "How many are we missing?"

Heather showed him the manifest. "That's not possible," he said. "You must have missed some." A drop of cold sweat trickled down his back. It was bad enough to have only ten-thousand marchers when he had promised Dickens several times that. But to only have five thousand people show up? His career as a march organizer would be over before it started. He nearly yanked the clipboard out of Heather's hands. "Let me see the phone list. I'll make some calls."

His desperation increased as he went down the list. Lots of people were on vacation. Others couldn't make the trip because their kids were already back in school. And a fair number of folks admitted to dropping out because one god or another had made a house call and had made a believer out of them – not a believer in his One True God, but in that fake Jesus who showed up in Colorado and started this whole mess.

He handed the clipboard back to Heather, feeling defeated. "I just don't know what to do, sugar lips," he said. "It's such a small crowd. We'll hardly make a dent."

"Milton," she said, "don't flake out on me now. The TV cameras are already there. They are expecting a show, and we are going to give them one. Come on." She grabbed his arm and started pulling him toward the start of the march.

Their route took them past the bag check table, where there was still a line. "Can't you speed this up?" Harkness asked the police. "We need to get going, and these people all need to come with us."

"Then you should have told your people to leave their weapons at home," the officer said, gesturing toward a tub where an assortment of guns was piling up. "Doesn't matter if they have a concealed-carry permit from their home state," he went on. "They can't carry a firearm in the District unless they have a D.C. permit."

"We did tell them," Milton said, backing off. "Sorry, officer."

"And then we run into jokers like this guy," the officer continued, hooking a thumb at the man whose backpack was currently being searched. A number of his belongings were already piled on the table – a cap gun, a toy bow and arrow, and some firecrackers. The cop tossed the firecrackers in the bin with the guns.

"Aw, man," the guy said.

The cop kept digging. "What's this for?" he said, pulling out an Indian war bonnet that looked like it had come from a Halloween costume.

"Me heap big Indian. Me go on warpath," the man said, and then popped his hand against his mouth several times. "Woo woo woo woo woo!"

The cop rolled his eyes and handed the thing back to the man. "Go on, get out of here," he said. "Next." The man grinned and walked off, waving at Harkness as if he knew him.

"Friend of yours?" the officer next to him inquired.

"No," Harkness said, baffled, although the man did seem familiar somehow. "Thank you, officer. Just do the best you can." He tried to get another look at the man who had waved to him, but he had been swallowed up by the crowd.

Heather squeezed his arm. "Let's go get the crowd stirred up, honey."

"Right, right," he said, distracted, and allowed her to lead him to the front of the line.

The paths around the Tidal Basin were surprisingly well-traveled in the early-morning hours. Darrell and his men tried to look inconspicuous, but it was hard to do, given that all twenty-five of them were in fatigues and each carried an assault rifle. One runner kept glancing at them as he ran up and down the steps of the memorial several times. He stopped, finally, and took a long pull from a water bottle. "You guys doing a drill today?" he asked as he stretched.

"That's right," Darrell responded.

"Well, enjoy," the man said before he ran off again.

Darrell grunted. *Enjoyment* was not the word he would have used. He was beginning to regret not having stopped for breakfast; his stomach felt like it was eating itself. But it was always that way before a mission.

At last, Terry looked at his watch. "It's 0900," he said.

Darrell nodded and motioned to his men. "Move out. Double time." They set out at a run.

"It's nine o'clock," Heather said to Harkness. Then she turned to the crowd and yelled, "Let's go, everybody! It's time!" They stepped out smartly across 14th Street, a police cordon holding up traffic for them. Half the group was chanting, "We believe in the One True God," and other half yelled, "Indians go home!" The man with the Halloween headdress capered alongside the marchers, letting out a war whoop now and then.

Harkness had never felt so exhilarated in his life.

Sue heard her alarm and shut it off. Partly in trepidation and partly in relief, she began chanting again.

Lady Columbia, we ask You for Your aid.
Protect this place and keep all its people safe.

After the third time through, she added a little prayer of her own: "Goddess, help us. Gaia, be with me."

Tracie, Tess and Schuyler watched the coverage on their tiny monitor. Max and Antonia kicked things off. Then it was Heela's turn. She stood on a corner with the crowd seething past behind her. A man with a poor imitation of an Indian headdress danced around behind her, waving at the camera and grimacing.

"Jackass," Schuyler muttered.

"There's one in every crowd," Tess agreed. Then she looked more closely at the background behind the line of protestors. "Hey, look at that. Is the Washington Monument glowing?"

"Let's go see," Schuyler said. He struck out, down the path behind the museum, and the women followed him. "It sure looks like it's glowing, doesn't it?" he said when the women joined him on the 4th Street sidewalk. "Maybe it's the way the sun's reflecting off the stone."

Tracie looked behind them dubiously. Then she pointed to the top of the Capitol. "Look at the dome, you guys," she said. "The statue up there is glowing, too. And that can't be a trick of the light."

Schuyler turned on the camera and got shots of the phenomena. "I hope these turn out," he said. "Was it supposed to rain today? I didn't bring a cover for the camera."

Tess looked to the west again; beyond the Washington Monument, a wall of dark clouds was building. She began to wonder just exactly what Sue and her group had conjured up.

Chapter 18

As the march passed 7th Street, the fake Indian danced north, between the Hirschhorn and the Air and Space museums, and out of sight. Some of the protestors noticed, but assumed the man would join up with them again later.

Darrell's platoon reached the National Museum of the American Indian just ahead of the protestors. He yelled to his men to spread out along the sidewalk in front of the museum entrance. Then he recognized Sue. He clapped her on the shoulder and gave her a grim smile as he passed her. She grabbed at his sleeve and pointed at the statue at the very top of the Capitol. It looked as if a green spotlight had been trained on it. "Columbia has been roused," Sue said. "We're not alone."

I don't know what the hell you're talking about, but okay. He smiled uncertainly at her. "Maybe you should go inside and get out of the sun," he said.

"Not yet," she said. "I want to see this."

He touched her shoulder again and joined his men.

"Here they come," Tess said as the noise level increased. Schuyler shouldered the camera and the three of them approached the street. As they crossed the plaza in front of the museum, a group of people – several of them dressed in elaborately beaded, feathered costumes – came out through the front doors. With a pang, she realized they were probably Darrell's friends. She refused to let herself search their faces; she wouldn't have known Ruthie if she'd tripped over her, and anyway, she had a job to do.

She turned to the street again, and her stomach lurched; Darrell was one of the troops in riot gear standing along the sidewalk. Schuyler had already pushed past him to get a shot of the marchers approaching the museum.

"Schuyler!" she yelled, and Darrell turned his head. Their eyes met for a second – his hardened and battle-weary, hers guarded. Then he turned around again.

Sue looked to be in some sort of ecstasy. She kept pointing at the top of the Capitol. Tess shot her a thumbs-up and yelled again at Schuyler.

Finally he returned, shouldering past Darrell again. Then daylight dawned. "Hey, is that...?"

"Yes," said Tess shortly.

"They're going to call for us," Tracie scolded him. "You need to stick with us."

"We needed shots of the front of the march," he grumbled as he handed each of them an earpiece.

"Tess, can you hear me?" Tracie said in her ear as soon as she had the thing in place. She nodded. Tracie paused, listening hard to some chatter Tess couldn't make out. "Okay, they're coming to you in five."

"Shit," muttered Schuyler, fiddling with a setting.

"Come on!" Tess hissed. "We don't have time!"

"Go," was all he said, just as the air signal came up in her earpiece.

"Tess Showalter is at the museum," Max was saying. "Tess, what's it look like there?"

"Max, all here is in readiness," she began. "The museum staff has been on alert for days, as you know, and security here has been tripled." She had gleaned that tidbit the day before. "To my right, if we can get a shot of the street...." Schuyler obligingly panned left while she kept talking. "You can see the police presence – D.C. police across the street are patrolling the intersections, and here at the museum itself, there appears to be a cordon of military troops guarding the entrance. Also, you can see a few ordinary citizens. I believe they're part of a Pagan coalition which conducted a ritual early this morning here on the Mall, lending their protection, and that of their gods, to today's events. And unless I'm mistaken, here on the plaza next to me are some of the people who will be performing at the Earth festival at the museum today. Is that right, sir?"

Schuyler panned back to her as she approached one of the men in costume and stuck her mic in his face.

"Uh, yeah, that's right," the man said. He wore a denim shirt with beaded leggings; a bustle of feathers was attached at the small of his back. "We're dancers from the Pokagon Band of Potawatomi Indians."

"And you've come from where to perform here today?"

"Michigan. Southern Michigan."

"Did you expect any of this when you agreed to come?"

"We heard there was going to be a protest, but we didn't realize how big a deal it would be until we got here." He glanced nervously toward the street

"If you had the chance to talk to one of these marchers, one on one, what would you say?" Tess asked. Schuyler was giving her the signal to wrap it up, but she ignored him.

"I would try to make him understand that we're all connected," the man said. "All the peoples of the Earth are connected. The human people, the animal people, the plant people – we're all connected, and we all just want to live in peace. The only thing we want from these people coming up the street toward us right now is respect."

"That's all any of us wants," Tess said. "Thank you, sir, and good luck with your performance today. Max, back to you."

"And we're out," Schuyler said.

"Can I get your name?" asked Tess. "Sorry, I should have asked you while we were on the air."

"I'd rather not give my name, if that's okay with you," he said. "In case some of these folks decide to come after us, I don't want them to be able to track down me and my family too easily."

Tess let out a breath. "Understood. Okay, well, thanks for talking with me."

"Sure," he said.

While they had talked, the vanguard of the march had reached the museum. Now, from the street, someone yelled, "Hey, there's some of those Indians!" and the crowd surged toward the plaza.

"Hold the line!" Darrell roared, and his men moved to stand shoulder to shoulder.

"Let's get 'em!" one of the men in the street hollered.

The dancers huddled against the doors, pounding on them to be let in. Tess realized that with the museum's opening still an hour away, the doors were probably locked from the inside. And the guards would be reluctant to push a door open for them in case a protestor got into the museum behind them.

She glanced at Schuyler; he had the camera running, taking it all in. "Tracie!" she shouted. "Tell them it's happening! Tell them to come back to me!"

There was some garble in her ear; the ambient noise level made it hard to hear. But she heard Antonia say her name, so she started talking. "Antonia, the protestors have reached the museum and they're trying to break through the line of troops, but the line is holding so far...."

Out of the corner of her eye, she caught a flash of color. A man in an obviously fake Indian headdress walked confidently past her. She only registered that he was holding a gun when he raised it to his shoulder and began firing into the crowd.

The roar increased as the protestors surged against the cordon of officers. Tess kept talking into her mic, explaining that the Indian with the gun had come out of nowhere.

Then one of the troops fell. Tess heard Darrell screaming, "Hold your fire!" But someone must not have been able to hold back, for a shot whizzed past her.

"We have to move!" Tess screamed into the mic, and the three of them jumped back just as the protestors surged through the gap left by the fallen man.

The fake Indian had disappeared. The real Indians ran — down the path behind the museum and past the waterfall to 4th Street — with the mob of protestors in hot pursuit.

"Go!" Tracie said. "I'll stay here with our stuff!"

"Come on!" Schuyler yelled, and he and Tess took off, Tess cursing herself for a fool. She could have stopped the gunman who started it all. *He walked right past me. I could have caught him, tackled him, as soon as I saw he had the gun. But no — I had to be the big TV star. I had to keep running my mouth. And now maybe somebody is dead.*

Sue saw everyone running and realized exactly where they would end up — bouncing back and forth between her wind turbines and overrunning her demonstration house. With a beseeching glance toward Columbia, she dodged the crowd trying to fit down the narrow path behind the museum by running up 3rd Street instead.

Darrell was moving before he realized it. After his relations he ran, trying to catch up to them before anyone else got hurt.

Over and over, his mind replayed his buddy Terry falling beside him, bleedig from a hole in his forehead. They had been together at Al-Laqbah. *We survived that hellhole, only to fall into this one.*

"Warren! Report!" his radio yelled.

Darrell hit the switch as he ran. "It's FUBAR, sir." *Just as we feared it would be.* "One man down. We're in pursuit."

"Understood. We'll rendezvous on the Mall."

Darrell nodded as he and his men reached 4th Street. He saw movement through the trees and ran toward it, his gun in his hand, his men following.

In seconds, he was on the Mall, yelling at the bystanders milling around to get to cover. Then he saw Ruthie and stopped, as his men ran past him and waded into the crowd.

She was standing on the sidewalk, on the periphery of the melee. Near her in the grass was a young man – a kid, really – with an orange backpack. The kid had taken off the pack and was fishing in it for something. He withdrew a large bottle, opened it, and lobbed it toward the crowd.

Darrell got a whiff as it flew past him and shattered at Ruthie's feet. *Almonds,* his brain registered. *Cyanide.* In a split second, he ticked through what he knew of the chemical agent: dangerous at close range, but the fumes rise rapidly and disperse quickly in open places. "Move back!" he shouted. "Everybody move back! Clear the area now now now!" But no one could hear him.

Then Ruthie fell.

He had to help her.

He couldn't touch her. He was in charge – he couldn't afford to be poisoned, too.

He shoved the gun away from him and, raising his arms to the heavens, cried out to the Air Spirits to blow away the poison and save these poor humans. Four times, he repeated his cry. He didn't even realize he was wailing in Potawatomi.

Tess, trailing Schuyler across the grass, recognized the kid who tossed the bottle. He was the same one they had surprised in Sue's office – the same one who had approached Sue before the shouting started.

He hesitated just long enough to see the woman fall, and then took two steps back as Darrell began crying to the heavens.

Her panic was rising. This wasn't her place; this wasn't her battle. She was too weak, too insignificant. And besides, her journalistic training told her not to get involved. She should be focused on the story, on getting the shots.

She sucked in a breath, willing herself to stay calm. *Just stop it. You let one troublemaker get past you today, and people were hurt because of it. Nobody saw this guy except you and Darrell, and Darrell's busy. You are not just the best person to do this – you are the ONLY ONE.*

Resolutely, she pulled on her mental mask.

As crows clamored in her ears and with Morrigan lending her strength, Tess raced across the grass and tackled the kid. He struggled to free himself with his face in the dirt, but she held on. "You're not going anywhere, you bastard," she said, her voice hoarse. Then she heard rumbling, and looked up.

Sue, too, looked up. Her wind turbines were spinning much faster than they should ever have been; the blades were a solid blur. Throwing formality to the ever-increasing winds, she simply cried, "Gaia, help me!"

The goddess answered as dark clouds boiled out of both east and west. Sue felt power surge up through her feet. In ecstasy, she raised her hands. A bolt of green fire shot from her left hand and attached itself to the statue atop the Capitol; from her right, a bolt of dazzling white sped to the top of the Washington Monument. At Gaia's whispered command, she brought her hands together with a resounding crack of thunder, then threw the joined lightning up. It struck the protective dome the Pagans had created, lighting the whole scene for a moment with an eerie glow.

As it faded, the rain poured down.

The rain called Darrell back from his trance. Blinking water from his eyes, he saw the kid with the backpack pinned to the ground – with Tess, of all people, sitting on top of him. The D.C. cops had moved in and were arresting protestors right and left. His relations had gathered off to one side, their regalia getting soaked while more D.C. cops were talking to them. On the other side of the crowd, Paulsen was rounding up Darrell's platoon.

He knew he should report to his C.O. But first he had to check on Ruthie.

She was still unconscious. Paramedics had already arrived; someone in the police force had apparently had the presence of mind to have them on standby. One was ripping off her outer clothing and stuffing it into a hazmat bag while the other washed her exposed skin.

"Ruthie," he croaked, his hand reaching toward her.

"Don't touch her," the paramedic warned through his mask. "We need to get her to the hospital." Two seconds more, and they had her loaded onto a gurney and into the ambulance.

As the siren spun up, he noticed Tess standing beside him. She peered up at him through the downpour. "Was that her?"

He nodded.

"I thought so. Is she gonna be okay?"

He shrugged and looked after the ambulance again. "I don't know. She was right on top of it when it hit." Then he turned back to her. "You tackled him?"

"Yeah," Tess said with a wondering laugh. "I saw the little shit throw the bottle and then start moving away. Then you yelled for everybody to get back, so..." She shrugged. "Who knew I had it in me?" After another moment, she said, "I could've had the gunman, too. He walked right past me, you know? Right before he started firing." She shook her head. "I couldn't let this one get away."

He put his arm around her. "Thank you."

"Ahh," she said with a half-shrug. "What are friends for?" But she clung to him, burying her face in his shirt for a moment.

"Warren!" his C.O. yelled.

For the second time that day, he had to abandon a woman he cared about. "I've got to go," he said, pulling away from her.

"That's okay," she said, wiping her eyes with the heel of one hand. "I should do another live shot."

"Where's your camera guy?"

She snorted. "Probably inside somewhere. He didn't think to bring a rain cover for the camera." She looked up at him. "See you at home."

"Warren!" Paulsen barked again.

"Aye, sir," he called. Then he ducked his head in a sort of bow to Tess, and trotted off through the rain to join his men.

Chapter 19

"They're not damaged," the contractor said wonderingly. Sue had called him in on a weekend, overtime budget be damned, to assess the effects of the previous day's events. He had spent the last hour climbing inside the monstrous things to check them out.

"So revving them up like that didn't hurt them?"

He shook his head, the corners of his mouth turned down. "None of the motors burned out. And the electronics are fine, too. It's like...magic, or something."

"Or something," she agreed, remembering the feel of lightning dancing on her hands.

"Although I did spot one unintended consequence," he said.

"Oh?"

"Yeah. These babies generated so much power yesterday that Pepco owes you big money."

She laughed. "We'll be able to put that to good use."

For the second day in a row, Darrell found himself driving into D.C. before sunrise.

He had been unable to fall asleep the night before, his brain buzzing with the events of the day just past. When he had finally rejoined his unit, Paulsen said nothing to him about his odd performance. He'd simply asked, "Friend of yours?"

Darrell had nodded. "My wife."

Paulsen knew damn well Darrell was divorced, but he didn't say anything about the missing *ex*. With a grunt, he had ordered the men back to the Tidal Basin.

But once they'd stowed the kayaks back at the marina, Paulsen had pulled him aside briefly. "We'll talk Monday. Get some rest."

Darrell couldn't wait for *that* conversation.

In the meantime, he needed to see Ruthie.

He arrived well in advance of visiting hours. He stopped at a coffee shop across from the hospital to while away the time, idly checking his phone and trying to still the impatience and worry in his heart.

Then a bleary-eyed Mike stumbled in the door. He spotted Darrell immediately, and they embraced. "You're up early, too, I see," Darrell said.

"Couldn't sleep. They wouldn't let us in to see Ruthie yesterday. I'm hoping they'll let us in today."

"I hope so, too," Darrell said. The thought that he might not be able to see her had never occurred to him.

"Coffee," Mike said. "Need anything?"

Direction. Explanations. Solace. He waved his cousin off. "Nah, I'm good."

His cousin seemed to hear his unvoiced thoughts. He squeezed Darrell's shoulder and went up to order.

When he returned, he brought a couple of breakfast sandwiches with him. "You need to eat," he said.

"Not hungry," Darrell muttered, but he ate his anyway.

"So," Mike said. "That thing you did yesterday." Darrell squirmed as his cousin went on, "You actually called the Air Spirits, didn't you? I didn't mishear that, did I?"

"No, you didn't mishear it. And before you ask, no, I don't know how I did it."

"That's some powerful medicine," Mike said, his voice low. "We could sure use that at home."

Darrell sighed. "I am given to understand," he said, "that I am right where the gods want me to be."

Mike waited.

Darrell sighed again. "Look, Mike. I won't pull any punches with you. I hate it here. I hate the Navy and everything it's put me through." He thought briefly of Al-Laqbah and winced. "I hate who I've become since I joined up. The blessing ceremony two nights ago was the most genuine and alive I have felt since...." He raised one hand, palm up, as if the gesture finished his sentence.

"But," he went on, "if I hadn't been here yesterday – not as a dancer or a *midew*, but as a man with a gun – if I hadn't been here yesterday to do what I did, all of you might be in the hospital. Ruthie might be dead."

Mike frowned. "I don't get it. You didn't need the gun for what you did."

"But I needed the battle experience to call forth that power," Darrell said, the realization coming clear as he talked it through. "I needed those emotions. That anger. The hair-trigger reactions." He looked away for a moment. "I don't know how to explain it any better." *Other than to say that Nanabush was right, damn it.* "But I needed to be who I am now in order to do what I did."

Mike's lips quirked. "So you're a Potawatomi superhero? That's cool. I'll get the kids working on a graphic novel about you."

Darrell ducked his head to hide his grin. Then he checked his phone. "Hey, I think we can go in now."

The nurse allowed them in, after Darrell said Ruthie was his wife. "But only for a few minutes," the nurse said. "She's still pretty sick."

Ruthie was awake when they entered. Darrell thought she looked like hell – and at the same time, she looked like the dearest thing in the world to him. "Hi, guys," she said.

Mike took her hand while Darrell leaned over and kissed her forehead. "How are you feeling?" Darrell asked.

"I've been better." She smiled a little. "But the doctor said I should be able to go home in a day or two. I'm okay – just really tired."

"That's good news," Mike said with relief. "Really good news."

But Darrell's heart sunk. He knew enough about chemical warfare to know she was probably lying. He turned to Mike. "You guys are supposed to take off for home today, right? Why don't you go ahead and go? I'll take care of getting her home."

"Well," Mike said, "I do have to go to work tomorrow, and so do some of the others."

"Good. It's settled." His gaze refocused on Ruthie.

Mike must have read the expression on Darrell's face, because he said, "Why don't I leave you two alone. I'll be back later with the rest of the gang." He squeezed Ruthie's hand. "Glad to hear you're on the mend."

"See you later, Mike," she called as he let himself out. Then she looked back at Darrell.

"Why didn't you tell him the truth?" he asked.

"I couldn't." She began crying silently. "The doctor said they don't know yet how extensive...."

He longed to sweep her up from the bed and hold her. Instead, he put his forehead against hers. "I'll be here for you," he said. "I promise."

She took a deep breath and coughed. "No," she said.

He pulled back. "What?"

She had stopped crying, but tears still glistened in tracks on her cheeks. "I said no." She put her hands on his shoulders and pushed him upright.

"But I don't...."

"Darrell, honey," she sighed. "I will always cherish what we had. But your life has turned into something I can't be part of any more."

Bewildered, he said, "What was Friday night about, then?"

"Friday night, I thought you'd changed. You were acting like the man I fell in love with."

"I *am* the man you fell in love with," he said.

"No," she said. "Yesterday reminded me of who you really are. The man I loved is still there, but there's a hard shell around him now, and he won't come out unless something terrible happens."

The man I loved. Past tense.

Darrell stood by her bedside for a long moment, his eyes cast down, looking at nothing. "If that's the way you want it," he said at last.

"It's not the way I want it," she said. "I've never wanted it this way. But this is the way it has to be."

He nodded. Then he stroked her cheek one last time, and gave her a lingering kiss. "Goodbye, Ruthie," he whispered.

"Goodbye, Darrell." She closed her eyes.

As he walked back to his car, Nanabush appeared beside him.

"Get the fuck away from me," Darrell snarled.

"Okay, okay. We'll talk later."

"I guess I don't have a choice, do I?" Darrell said bitterly. But the god was gone.

Tess was standing in the kitchen, stuffing down a sandwich, when Darrell came in the back door. She took in his hunched shoulders and ravaged face and said, "God, you look like hell."

Wordlessly, he went downstairs.

"Probably should have phrased it better," she muttered. She thought about following him to apologize, but then she glanced at her phone and said, "Shit." She had just barely enough time to get to the debrief meeting at work.

She wasn't particularly looking forward to it. The coverage had been stellar, she knew, but she fully expected a dressing-down from Antonia for not sticking with the story. Heela had had to do the final live shot; the police were still questioning Tess.

As she entered the newsroom, however, the assembled staff rose to their feet and applauded. She stopped dead in the doorway, knowing her mouth had dropped open.

"Our hero!" Antonia sang out, and gave her a hug.

"God, Antonia," Tess said as people resumed their seats. "I thought you were gonna fire me."

That got a laugh. "How could I?" she said. "You rounded up a domestic terrorist."

Tess blinked. "What?"

"Haven't you been watching the news this morning? The cops found a bunch of chemicals in the basement of his parents' house in McLean. Not just cyanide, but ricin."

"Oh, my God," Tess said. "No, I hadn't heard."

"And apparently he was trying to make sarin gas, or something similar," Antonia went on. "He's a real nutjob. Good work, Tess." She beamed. Then she turned to the room at large, "If anybody ever asks you why we spend the money on an investigative unit?" She held a hand out in Tess's direction. "Right here."

Finding her feet at last, Tess Showalter – Network Correspondent Woman, Seeker of Truth – curtseyed to her colleagues as their applause erupted again.

Dickens and Quinn stood together on one of the Capitol's balconies, watching the grounds crew disassemble the unused dais. The march had never gotten that far; police broke it up after the altercation on the Mall. Harkness and that Willis woman had escaped arrest, but he expected that to be rectified shortly.

"At least we're rid of that dead wood," Dickens remarked.

"I said all along it was a mistake to align ourselves with deniers," Quinn said, nearly spitting the word. "Too unstable. You need rock-solid people you can rely on to pull off something like this."

"Gentlemen, gentlemen," said a voice behind them.

Dickens turned to regard the shadowy figure; just once, he'd like to see the man's face. "You played your part well," he said. "That Indian headdress was a stroke of genius."

"It was, wasn't it?" the man preened. "I must thank you, Quinn, for secreting the weapon as I requested."

Quinn nodded. "No problem. Plenty more where that came from."

Dickens ventured, "So have we convinced you now that the deniers and the anti-Native crowd are not our natural allies?"

"Oh, I wouldn't say that," the man said. "But we won't be teaming up with them again for a while. I needed a sacrificial victim for this maneuver, and they were convenient."

"What's our next target?" Quinn asked.

"I think we'll be heading south," the man said. "I know that will please you."

"It does," Quinn said. "Anything that will shore up my firm's funding base, I am all in favor of."

"And anything that keeps money flowing to the military keeps my political party in business," Dickens chimed in.

"Very good," the man said. "Then shall we let loose the dogs of war?"

Darrell considered not answering his phone, but he rolled over anyway and checked who it was. Then he sat up and took the call. "Warren."

"Darrell, it's Wes Paulsen." His C.O. sounded tired. "I was going to wait 'til tomorrow morning to talk to you, but something's come up."

"Sir?"

"Look." Paulsen was silent for a moment. "I don't know exactly how you did what you did yesterday, and frankly, I don't want to know. I was perfectly happy not believing in anything at all, until the Second Coming bollixed it all up for me." Paulsen took an audible breath. "Anyway, I think it would be best if you took a break from your duties at the Pentagon for a little while."

"Sir?" Darrell said again.

"I'm reassigning you temporarily to Little Creek," Paulsen went on. "You are to report to Commander McGuire on August 28th. That gives you two weeks to pack up what you'll need for the next month and get down there."

"Sir, I don't understand."

"McGuire will brief you," he continued. "All I know is Naval Intelligence intercepted a communique indicating that Hampton Roads may come under a terrorist attack sometime in the next month."

"But sir," Darrell said. "Why me?"

Paulsen was silent for a moment, as if choosing his words carefully. "From what I've been told," he said, "this mission may require someone with your, uh, special talents."

So you're a Potawatomi superhero now?

Darrell groaned inwardly. "Understood, sir." Although he didn't understand at all, really, and he had no idea how he was expected to help.

"Good," Paulsen said. "Feel free to access the office today to collect anything you think you might need down there. And Darrell...."

"Sir?"

"I'm doing you a favor, son," his C.O. said. "The alternative would have been letting the medics poke and prod at you for a few weeks, to try to figure out what makes you tick."

Darrell winced. "Sounds unpleasant."

"It wouldn't tickle. On the bright side," he said, more cheerfully, "maybe with you out of Washington, it'll all blow over. And you know these terrorist reports hardly ever amount to anything. Just think of it as a month-long vacation at the beach."

"Sounds like just the ticket, sir," Darrell said.

Heather was furious. "Milton!" she yelled. "We need to be out of here *today*, not next week!"

"Coming, honey," he said, puffing, as he carried another box full of her shoes to the waiting luggage cart. He stacked it atop the teetering pile already there and said, "That's the last of it. Now we just need to get it loaded into our car, and..."

"*Whose* car?" she said. "That car is *mine*, you wretch. You came into this deal with nothing, remember? Everything was mine except the clothes on your back. Which you can keep."

"But honey," he began.

"Don't you 'honey' me," she said, getting in his face. She had a good inch of height on him in these heels, which, right now, pleased her very much.

"Children, children," said a new voice in the apartment behind them.

Their heads jerked as one. "Who...oh, my God," Heather said. Her mouth dropped open.

"Not you again!" said Harkness.

"Yes, Milton," Jesus said. "Me again."

"How did you get in here?" Harkness demanded, while Heather sunk to her knees. "Where's the projector? Where's the harness?" He glanced down at her. "What are you doing down there? Get up! He's not really Jesus. He's that faker from Colorado."

Jesus shook His head. "You know who I am, don't you, Heather?"

"Forgive me!" she sobbed, prostrating herself. "I didn't know!"

She felt His touch on the crown of her head. "I know," He said. "It's so easy for people to be led astray. My Father and I forgive you your doubt."

She sat up and wiped her cheeks. She knew her makeup must be running, but...this was Jesus! He would forgive her raccoon eyes. He had already forgiven her for her doubt. "And I'm sorry, too," she said tremulously, "for all the trouble we've caused."

"Alas," He said, "for that, you will have to earn forgiveness."

"Wh-what do you mean?"

"You, Heather, were the driving force behind the march," said Jesus. "It never would have happened if you hadn't stepped up to organize it and keep Milton on track. And because of your actions, one person is dead and another is seriously injured. You will have to answer for that to the Earthly authorities."

In the distance, she thought she heard sirens. Her shoulders sagged.

"Now see here," Harkness began babbling.

"Shut up, Milton," she said. "You're only making things worse for yourself."

"No, *you* shut up, Heather," he said, with savage glee. She was surprised; she hadn't thought he had it in him to stand up to her. "I need proof that this man is who he says he is." He turned back to Jesus. "Do a miracle for me. Change water into wine. Bring somebody back to life. Something." He fluttered his hands, and then folded his arms and glared at Him.

The Son of God had a twinkle in his eye. "Okay. If you say so." He waved His hand, and with a *pop*, Harkness disappeared.

Heather stared at the spot where Harkness had been. Then she turned to Jesus. "Did You send him to Hell?" she asked timidly.

"In a manner of speaking," He said. "The only Hell is the one you make for yourself. But he's not going to be happy about where I've sent him." He held out a hand, and she took it. "I'll take care of getting your things home to your parents," He said as she rose.

"Thank You," she said fervently.

He regarded her kindly. "Turn your heart to the Light, Heather," He said. "That will be thanks enough for Me." He faded out, taking all her boxes with Him.

A peremptory knock sounded on the door. "Police!"

She took a tissue from her purse and dabbed carefully at her eyes before she opened the door. "I'm ready," she said.

Milton stared at the barren landscape around him. "Oh, no," he moaned. "Not here. *Anywhere* but here."

"Milton!" called someone behind him. That voice confirmed it; he really had been sent to the Indian mission in South Dakota. He turned, sagging, as Father Louis emerged from Holy Rosary Church and shook his hand. "It's good to see you! You must be out of prison, then."

"Hello, Father," he said dully. "Yes, I've been out for a few years now."

"Well, what have you been doing? We'll have to catch up." The Jesuit priest glanced at the empty parking lot. "How did you get up here to Pine Ridge, anyway? Did someone drop you off?"

Harkness barked a laugh. "You could say that." Then he sobered as the realization hit him: real Jesus or no, the man had given him a second chance to get things right.

Father Louis must have seen the shifting expressions on his face. "Is there something I can do for you, Milton?" he asked gently.

"Father," Harkness said with wonder in his voice, "I seem to have lost my way. Can you help me?"

The priest's smile was like a shaft of sunlight cutting through the darkness. "I thought you'd never ask," he said, and held the door of the church open for him.

Author's Note

It's amazing how you can live somewhere but never really know the place. I've lived in the D.C. area for more than twenty years, and still I had to do research for this book. In particular, I needed help with street names around the National Mall (which is not a shopping center – I hope I made that clear!) and with the interior of the Hart Office Building. All I can say is, thank the gods for the Architect of the Capitol's website (http://www.aoc.gov/) and Google Earth.

I'm also learning quite a bit about the Potawatomi for this series. As their spiritual beliefs are quite similar to those of the Ojibwe, I found the following books by Basil Johnston to be invaluable: *Ojibway Ceremonies* (University of Nebraska Press, 1990), *Ojibway Heritage* (University of Nebraska Press, 1990), *The Manitous: The Spiritual World of the Ojibway* (Minnesota Historical Society Press, 2001) and *Honour Earth Mother* (University of Nebraska Press, 2004).

As usual, it's taken a village to get this book out the door. Once again, my thanks go out to Susan Strayer and Kat Milyko for their editorial assistance. Thanks, too, to Kriss Morton at the Finishing Fairies for orchestrating the book launch. And a huge thank-you to my fellow minions at Indies Unlimited, and to my buddies in the BookGoodies authors' group on Facebook. Y'all rock!

If you enjoyed this book, won't you please go back to the place where you bought it and leave a review? Thank you!

Lynne Cantwell
November 2013

Glossary

The words and phrases used in the text come from a booklet called "Conversational Potawatomi," written for the Citizen Potawatomi Nation's language classes, and from an online Potawatomi dictionary.

bozho: hello
nitawes: cousin
Ni je na?: How are you?
iwgwien: thank you
midew: a medicine man
Midewewin: medicine society
Bama mine: Later again. (See you later.)
Anwe she shena: I am fine.

About the Author

Lynne Cantwell is the author of eight fantasy novels. She is also a contributing author for Indies Unlimited. In a previous life, she was a broadcast journalist who worked at Mutual/NBC Radio News, CNN, and a bunch of other places you have probably never heard of. She has a master's degree in fiction writing from Johns Hopkins University. Currently, she lives near Washington, D.C.

Facebook:
http://www.facebook.com/pages/Lynne-Cantwell
Twitter:
http://twitter.com/lynnecantwell
Smashwords:
http://www.smashwords.com/profile/view/lynnecantwell
Goodreads:
http://www.goodreads.com/author/show/696603.Lynne_Cantwell
Blog:
http://hearth-myth.blogspot.com

TURN THE PAGE FOR A PREVIEW OF
UNDERTOW,
BOOK TWO OF THE
LAND, SEA, SKY TRILOGY!

Darrell tapped impatiently on the steering wheel as afternoon rush-hour traffic gathered around him. His timing was bad, and he knew it. He didn't have to report to his new command in Virginia Beach for another whole week. He could have stayed home in Alexandria for another night, or even two or three.

But enforced idleness had never been his style. Even when he was growing up in southern Michigan, he was always busy doing something – fishing or hiking, taking care of the family pets, shoveling snow from neighbors' sidewalks in winter, or helping his parents around the house. If there was some kind of active pursuit available, he was the first to step up and do it.

That had usually worked in his favor. His mentor back home, Gus, noticed him and recommended that he be trained as a *midew* – a medicine man for the Potawatomi Indian band they were both part of. And even though that training required periods of meditation and observation, he still felt like he was doing something.

Then he'd joined the Navy and learned the meaning of the phrase, "hurry up and wait." Navy life seemed like an exercise in suspended animation, with occasional furious bouts of reacting on instinct to a real or perceived threat.

But even that wasn't as bad as the past week had been.

Ever since the march organized by the European-American Rights Coalition and the Believers in the One True God – the one where his buddy Terry was killed by sniper fire in the middle of Washington, D.C., and where he cried out to the Air Spirits to save his ex-wife from cyanide poisoning – ever since that day, his life had been on hold. Ruthie was still hospitalized in Washington, recovering from her injuries, but she didn't want to see him. He was on the outs with his housemates, what with one thing and another. And his C.O. had temporarily reassigned him to Little Creek, but had given him two weeks off in the interim.

Darrell supposed Commander Paulsen had been trying to help. Paulsen certainly knew both Darrell and Terry had survived the Al-Laqbah massacre; maybe he wanted to give Darrell some time to get over his buddy's death. And too, Paulsen had an inkling of how much Ruthie had meant to Darrell; maybe he thought Darrell would appreciate having some free time to spend at her bedside. He might even have been grateful, if Ruthie had wanted him there.

More likely, though, Paulsen had considered Darrell a liability and simply wanted him to drop out of sight for a little while. Special Ops-trained personnel were supposed to be silent, deadly killers. On the Mall that day, crying to the heavens like some kind of Potawatomi superhero, Darrell had been anything but silent. Paulsen had even told him that the alternative to the transfer was to turn him over to the medics to see whether they could figure out how he could control the weather the way he had that day.

Darrell snorted. He wouldn't mind knowing the answer to that himself.

"What's so funny?" asked Nanabush, materializing in the passenger seat. The culture hero of Darrell's people wore lavishly-embroidered deerskin from his tunic to his moccasins, and a feathered roach adorned the back of his head. His ears were long and droopy like a bunny's, and his upper teeth protruded just a bit.

Darrell flicked a glance at the god. "Nothing. I was just thinking that even if the medics could figure out how I got those wind turbines to move so fast, they wouldn't tell me."

"They wouldn't have handed you over to the medics, My boy," Nanabush said, "no matter what your boss told you."

"You're probably right," Darrell said. "I probably would have ended up at Langley. Or Quantico."

Nanabush cocked his head. "Langley?"

"The CIA," Darrell elaborated. "And Quantico is the FBI."

"Ah. And I don't suppose they would have shared their findings with you, either."

"I wouldn't think so."

The god was silent for a moment, looking out at the passing scenery. "You've been here before, haven't you?"

Darrell nodded. "My first posting was at J. E. B. Little Creek."

"It will be like a sort of homecoming for you, then," the lop-eared god said slyly.

"There's nothing even vaguely homelike about a naval base," Darrell said. "It's a place that's dedicated to impermanence. Nobody ever settles down there. Everybody's always just passing through."

Nanabush fell silent again. At last, he said, "I'm sorry this has been so hard on you."

Resigned, Darrell lifted a hand from the wheel and let it fall. "It is what it is." He cut a look at Nanabush. "You're not thinking of letting me off the hook, are You?"

The god shook His head. "I can't. Everything We've heard indicates this next event is going to be even bigger than the last one."

"A bigger deal than that clusterfuck on the Mall? Hard to believe." *Us*, Darrell knew, meant the group of deities he had privately dubbed the God Squad: Nanabush, the Irish war goddess Morrigan, and the Wiccan Earth goddess Gaia. With occasional help from Diana, the Greek goddess of the hunt, and the Norse Trickster Loki, They were the eyes and ears of his human team in the spirit realm.

At least They were all still speaking to one another. Unlike his human teammates, who were kind of on the outs with him.

"So why *did* we leave so early?" Nanabush asked.

"Got sick of sitting around the house." Darrell changed lanes and swore; this lane wasn't moving any faster than the one he had just left.

"I thought we were going camping."

"We did go camping. Last weekend."

"I thought we were going for longer. You said you wanted to hike the Appalachian Trail."

Darrell sighed and shook his head. "Too much time with my own thoughts," he confessed. He had thought to hike the part of the A.T. that ran through Virginia – or a good chunk of it, at least. But most of the route follows a ridgetop, with little in the way of elevation gain. A pretty enough hike, and long, but it wouldn't have offered enough of a physical challenge to keep him from dwelling on his problems.

"So you think a week at the beach will give you less time to think?"

He gave the god as full a glance as he could manage while driving. "I need to find a place to stay down here," he said. "The Navy's not going to put me up for more than a few nights – I'll need something more permanent. This will give me time to do that."

"And less time to reconcile with Tess and Sue."

"That, too." Immersed in his own misery after Ruthie said goodbye to him, it took him a few days to realize Sue wasn't speaking to him. He traced it back to the conversation he'd had with her a couple of days before the march – about how she needed to get over the fact that he and Tess were seeing each other. About how she needed to stop playing the victim every time Tess got a boyfriend, and go out and find her own guys. He guessed she was still pissed off at him over that.

Of course, right afterward, Tess had also gotten pissed off at him and they had broken up. He thought maybe she had softened toward him – but then she realized Ruthie was in town, and got a clue about how much she still meant to Darrell. Things had been frosty between them since then.

"Well, you need to figure out a way," Nanabush admonished him. "We still need them on the team."

Darrell rolled his eyes. "Yeah, yeah. I will. It'll be fine. We just all need some time away from one another to cool off." He spoke with the intention of brushing off the god's concerns, but he realized that on some level, he was also trying to convince himself.

Nanabush grunted and fell silent.

Despite the heavy traffic, as they passed the exit for Mercury Boulevard, he felt his mood begin to lift. Things were beginning to look familiar. And despite his protestations, it would be nice to be back somewhere familiar – even if it wasn't really home.

As he rounded the final curve on the approach to the Hampton Roads Bridge-Tunnel, a pleased sigh escaped him. The sight of the Chesapeake Bay here, at its confluence with the James River, never failed to move him to happiness – especially on clear days like this one. He could never decide whether it was the expanse of sky, or the quality of the light as it reflected off the water, or if it was the bounty of the bay itself. But the air always seemed clearer, the water more cleansing, the very earth more welcoming.

He knew the truth, of course: he was surrounded by military installations. Just to the west, most of the aircraft carriers of the Navy's Sixth Fleet rode at anchor. Navy jets from Oceana and Dam Neck criss-crossed the skies so often that the locals barely noticed them. He had already passed the Army's Fort Eustis and the exit for Langley Air Force Base – a different Langley than the one in northern Virginia where the CIA had its headquarters, but named for the same man.

The region was awash in national defense as much, or more, as it was in natural beauty. And yet, the bay called to him. He was a sailor, after all, and the son of a people who lived as much on the Great Lakes as on land. He could look below the lethal surface layer and find his kinship with the water.

And then, at speed, he descended into the tunnel.

The Hampton Roads Bridge-Tunnel was not quite the marvel of engineering that its neighbor, the twenty-three-mile-long Chesapeake Bay Bridge-Tunnel, was. The whole structure here – bridges and tunnel, from the city of Hampton to Willoughby Spit – was only three and a half miles long. And yet it had great strategic importance, both for the Navy and for commercial shipping. The twin tunnels were engineered to span a natural trench 1 1/2 miles wide and about sixty feet deep. At its deepest point, Darrell knew, the road he drove on was more than a hundred feet below sea level.

He found himself drumming his fingers on the wheel again as traffic slowed in front of him. He knew drivers had a habit of slowing as they entered the tube full of artificial light after the sunshine outside. Some people had trouble crossing bridges, let alone a tunnel with tons of earth and water above them. But he had been on the road for hours. He was ready to get to his hotel and get out from behind the wheel for the day.

At last, he could see daylight ahead. Traffic sped up, hurtling now toward the light. He hoped it was a good omen for this trip, despite what Nanabush had said.

He glanced over at the empty passenger seat and realized the god had disappeared at some point. Darrell decided it was just as well. He didn't need any more complications in his life right now.